THE LAST HERO
A DISCWORLD FABLE

by TERRY PRATCHETT

illustrated by PAUL KIDBY

Also by Terry Pratchett

In Loving Memory

Old Vincent

First published in Great Britain 2001 by
Gollancz
A imprint of the Orion Publishing Group
Orion House, 5 Upper St Martin's Lane, London WC2H 9EA
An Hachette Livre UK Company

This edition published in Great Britian in 2007 by Gollancz

3 5 7 9 10 8 6 4 2

A CIP catalogue record for this book is available
from the British Library

ISBN 978 0 57508 1 963

Printed in Italy by Printer Trento

www.orionbooks.co.uk

The Orion Publishing Group's policy is to use papers that are natural, renewable and recyclable
products and made from wood grown in sustainable forests. The logging and manufacturing
processes are expected to conform to the environmental regulations of the country of origin.

The *place* where the story happened was a world on the back of four elephants perched on the shell of a giant turtle. That's the advantage of space. It's big enough to hold practically *anything*, and so, eventually, it does.

People think that it is strange to have a turtle ten thousand miles long and an elephant more than two thousand miles tall, which just shows that the human brain is ill-adapted for thinking and was probably originally designed for cooling the blood. It believes mere size is *amazing*.

There's nothing amazing about size. Turtles are amazing, and elephants are quite astonishing. But the fact that there's a big turtle is far less amazing than the fact that there is a turtle *anywhere*.

The *reason* for the story was a mix of many things. There was humanity's desire to do forbidden deeds merely because they were forbidden. There was its desire to find new horizons and kill the people who live beyond them. There were the mysterious scrolls. There was the cucumber. But mostly there was the knowledge that one day, quite soon, it would be all over.

'Ah, well, life goes on,' people say when someone dies. But from the point of view of the person who has just died, it doesn't. It's the universe that goes on. Just as the deceased was getting the hang of everything it's all whisked away, by illness or accident or, in one case, a cucumber. Why this has to be is one of the imponderables of life, in the face of which people either start to pray . . . or become really, really angry.

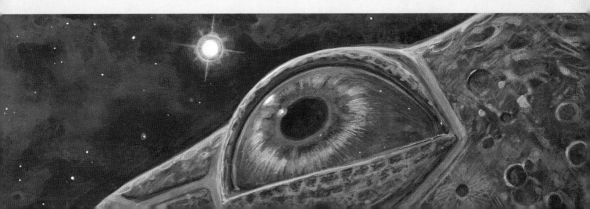

 he *beginning* of the story
happened tens of thousands
of years ago, on a wild and
stormy night, when a speck
of flame came down the mountain at
the centre of the world. It moved in
dodges and jerks, as if the unseen
person carrying it was sliding and
falling from rock to rock.

At one point the line became a streak
of sparks, ending in a snowdrift at the
bottom of a crevasse. But a hand thrust
up through the snow held the smoking
embers of the torch, and the wind,
driven by the anger of the gods, and
with a sense of humour of its own,
whipped the flame back into life . . .

And, after that, it never died.

he *end* of the story began high above the world, but got lower and lower as it circled down towards the ancient and modern city of Ankh-Morpork, where, it was said, anything could be bought and sold – and if they didn't have what you wanted they could steal it for you.

Some of them could even dream it . . .

The creature now seeking out a particular building below was a trained Pointless Albatross and, by the standards of the world, was not particularly unusual.* It was, though, pointless. It spent its entire life in a series of lazy journeys between the Rim and the Hub, and where was the point in that?

This one was more or less tame. Its beady mad eye spotted where, for reasons entirely beyond its comprehension, anchovies could be found. And someone would remove this uncomfortable cylinder from its leg. It seemed a pretty good deal to the albatross and from this it can be deduced that these albatrosses are, if not completely pointless, at least rather dumb.

Not at all like humans, therefore.

*Compared to, say, the Republican Bees, who committed rather than swarmed and tended to stay in the hive a lot, voting for more honey.

Ankh-Morpork

Flight has been been said to be one of the great dreams of Mankind. In fact it merely harks back to Man's ancestors, whose greatest dream was of falling off the branch. In any case, other great dreams of Mankind have included the one about being chased by huge boots with teeth. And no one says *that* one has to make sense.

Three busy hours later Lord Vetinari, the Patrician of Ankh-Morpork, was standing in the main hall of Unseen University, and he was impressed. The wizards, once they understood the urgency of a problem, and then had lunch, and argued about the pudding, could actually work quite fast.

Their method of finding a solution, as far as the Patrician could see, was by creative hubbub. If the question was, 'What is the best spell for turning a book of poetry into a frog?', then the one thing they would *not* do was look in any book with a title like *Major Amphibian Spells in a Literary Environment: A Comparison*. That would, somehow, be cheating. They would argue about it instead, standing around a blackboard, seizing the chalk from one another and rubbing out bits of what the current chalk-holder was writing before he'd finished the other end of the sentence. Somehow, though, it all seemed to work.

Now something stood in the centre of the hall. It looked, to the arts-educated Patrician, like a big magnifying glass surrounded by rubbish.

'Technically, my lord, an omniscope can see anywhere,' said Archchancellor Ridcully, who was technically the head of All Known Wizardry.*

'Really? Remarkable.'

'Anywhere *and* any time,' Ridcully went on, apparently not impressed himself.

'How extremely useful.'

'Yes, everyone says that,' said Ridcully, kicking the floor morosely. 'The trouble *is*, because the blasted thing can see *everywhere*, it's practically impossible to get it to see *anywhere*. At least, anywhere worth seeing. And you'd be amazed at how many places there are in the universe. And times, too.'

'Twenty past one, for example,' said the Patrician.

'Among others, indeed. Would you care to have a look, my lord?'

Lord Vetinari advanced cautiously and peered into the big round glass. He frowned.

'All I can see is what's on the other side of it,' he said.

'Ah, that's because it's set to *here* and *now*, sir,' said a young wizard who was still adjusting the device.

'Oh, I *see*,' said the Patrician. 'We have these at the palace, in fact. We call them *win-dows*.'

'Well, if I do *this*,' said the wizard, and did something to the rim of the glass, 'it looks the other way.' Lord Vetinari looked into his own face.

'And these we call *mir-rors*,' he said, as if explaining to a child.

'I think not, sir,' said the wizard. 'It takes a moment to realise what you're seeing. It helps if you hold up your hand . . .'

Lord Vetinari gave him a severe look, but essayed a little wave.

'Oh. How curious. What is your name, young man?'

'Ponder Stibbons, sir. The new Head of Inadvisably Applied Magic, sir. You see, sir, the trick isn't to *build* an omniscope because, after all, that's just a development of the old-fashioned crystal ball. It's to get it to see what you want. It's like tuning a string, and if—'

'Sorry, *what* applied magic?' said the Patrician.

'Inadvisably, sir,' said Ponder smoothly, as if hoping that he could avoid the problem by driving straight through it. 'Anyway . . . I think we can get it to the right area, sir. The power drain is considerable; we may have to sacrifice another gerbil.'

The wizards began to gather around the device.

'Can you see into the future?' said Lord Vetinari.

'In *theory*, yes, sir,' said Ponder. 'But that would be highly . . . well, inadvisable, you see, because initial studies indicate that the fact of observation would collapse the waveform in phase space.'

*That is, all those wizards who knew Archchancellor Ridcully, and were prepared to be led.

Not a muscle moved on the Patrician's face.

'Pardon me, I'm a little out-of-date on faculty staff,' he said. 'Are you the one who has to take the dried frog pills?'

'No, sir. That's the Bursar, sir,' said Ponder. 'He has to have them because he's insane, sir.'

'Ah,' said Lord Vetinari, and now he *did* have an expression. It was that of a man resolutely refraining from saying what was on his mind.

'What Mr Stibbons *means*, my lord,' said the Archchancellor, 'is that there are billions and billions of futures that, er, *sort of* exist, d'yer see? They're all . . . the possible *shapes* of the future. But apparently the first one you actually *look* at is the one that *becomes* the future. It might not be one you'd like. Apparently it's all to do with the Uncertainty Principle.'

'And that is . . . ?'

'I'm not sure. Mr Stibbons is the one who knows about that sort of thing.'

An orangutan ambled past, carrying an extremely large number of books under each arm. Lord Vetinari looked at the hoses that snaked from the omniscope and out through the open door and across the lawn to . . . what was it? . . . the High Energy Magic building?

He remembered the old days, when wizards had been gaunt and edgy and full of guile. They wouldn't have allowed an Uncertainty Principle to exist for any length of time; if you weren't certain, they'd say, what were you doing wrong? What you were uncertain of could kill you.

The omniscope flickered and showed a snowfield, with black mountains in the distance. The wizard called Ponder Stibbons appeared to be very pleased with this.

'I thought you said you could find him with this thing?' said Vetinari to the Archchancellor.

Ponder Stibbons looked up. 'Do we have something that he has owned? Some personal item he has left lying around?' he said. 'We could put it in the morphic resonator, connect that up to the omniscope and it'll home in on him like a shot.'

'Whatever happened to the magic circles and dribbly candles?' said Lord Vetinari.

'Oh, they're for when we're not in a hurry, sir,' said Ponder.

'Cohen the Barbarian is not known for leaving things lying around, I fear,' said the Patrician. 'Bodies, perhaps. All we know is that he is heading for Cori Celesti.'

'The mountain at the Hub of the world, sir? Why?'

'I was hoping you would tell me, Mr Stibbons. That's why I'm *here*.'

The Librarian ambled past again, with another load of books. Another response of the wizards, when faced with a new and unique situation, was to look through their libraries to see if it had ever happened before. This was, Lord Vetinari reflected, a good survival trait. It meant that in times of danger you spent the day sitting very quietly in a building with very thick walls.

He looked again at the piece of paper in his hand. Why were people so *stupid*? One sentence caught his eye: 'He says the last hero ought to return what the first hero stole.'

And, of course, *everyone* knew what the first hero stole.

Dunmanifestin

The gods play games with the fate of men. Not complex ones, obviously, because gods lack patience.

Cheating is part of the rules. And gods play hard. To lose all believers is, for a god, the *end*. But a believer who survives the game gains honour and extra belief. Who wins with the most believers, lives.

Believers can include other gods, of course. Gods *believe* in belief.

There were always many games going on in Dunmanifestin, the abode of the gods on Cori Celesti. It looked, from outside, like a crowded city.* Not all gods lived there, many of them being bound to a particular country or, in the case of the smaller ones, even one tree. But it was a Good Address. It was where you hung your metaphysical equivalent of the shiny brass plate, like those small discreet buildings in the smarter areas of major cities which nevertheless appear to house one hundred and fifty lawyers and accountants, presumably on some sort of shelving.

The city's domestic appearance was because, while people are influenced by gods, so gods are influenced by people.

Most gods were people-shaped; people don't have much imagination, on the whole. Even Offler the Crocodile God was only crocodile-*headed*. Ask people to imagine an animal god and they will, basically, come up with the idea of someone in a really bad mask. Men have been much better at inventing demons, which is why there are so many.

Above the wheel of the world, the gods played on. They sometimes forgot what happened if you let a pawn get all the way up the board.

*Few religions are definite about the size of Heaven, but on the planet Earth the Book of Revelation (ch. XXI, v.16) gives it as a cube 12,000 furlongs on a side. This is somewhat less than 500,000,000,000,000,000,000 cubic feet. Even allowing that the Heavenly Host and other essential services take up at least two-thirds of this space, this leaves about one million cubic feet of space for each human occupant – assuming that every creature that could be called 'human' is allowed in, and that the human race eventually totals a thousand times the number of humans alive up until now. This is such a generous amount of space that it suggests that room has also been provided for some alien races or – a happy thought – that pets are allowed.

t took a little longer for the rumour to spread around the city, but in twos and threes the leaders of the great Guilds hurried into the University.

Then the ambassadors picked up the news. Around the city the big semaphore towers faltered in their endless task of exporting market prices to the world, sent the signal to clear the line for high-priority emergency traffic, and then clack'd the little packets of doom to chancelleries and castles across the continent.

They were in code, of course. If you have news about the end of the world, you don't want *everyone* to know.

Lord Vetinari stared along the table. A lot had been happening in the past few hours.

'If I may recap, then, ladies and gentlemen,' he said as the hubbub died away, 'according to the authorities in Hunghung, the capital of the Agatean Empire, the Emperor Ghengiz Cohen, formerly known to the world as Cohen the Barbarian, is well en route to the home of the gods with a device of *considerable* destructive power and the intention, apparently, of, in his words, "returning what was stolen". And, in short, they ask us to stop him.'

'Why us?' said Mr Boggis, head of the Thieves' Guild. 'He's not *our* Emperor!'

'I understand the Agatean government believes us to be capable of anything,' said Lord Vetinari. 'We have zip, zing, vim and a go-getting, can-do attitude.'

'Can do what?'

Lord Vetinari shrugged. 'In this case, save the world.'

'But we'll have to save it for everyone, right?' said Mr Boggis. 'Even foreigners?'

'Well, yes. You cannot just save the bits you like,' said Lord Vetinari. 'But the thing about saving the world, gentlemen and ladies, is that it inevitably includes whatever you happen to be standing on. So let us move forward. Can magic help us, Archchancellor?'

'No. Nothing magical can get within a hundred miles of the mountain,' said the Archchancellor.

'Why not?'

'For the same reason you can't sail a boat into a hurricane. There's just *too much magic*. It overloads anything magical. A magic carpet would unravel in midair.'

'Or turn into broccoli,' said the Dean. 'Or a small volume of poetry.'

'Are you saying that we cannot get there in time?'

'Well . . . yes. Exactly. Of course. They're already near the base of the mountain.'

'And they're *heroes*,' said Mr Betteridge of the Guild of Historians.

'And that means, exactly?' said the Patrician, sighing.

'They're good at doing what they want to do.'

'But they are also, as I understand it, very old men.'

'Very old *heroes*,' the historian corrected him. 'That just means they've had a lot of *experience* in doing what they want to do.'

Lord Vetinari sighed again. He did not like to live in a world of heroes. You had civilisation, such as it was, and you had heroes.

'What exactly has Cohen the Barbarian done that is *heroic*?' he said. 'I seek only to understand.'

'Well . . . you know . . . heroic deeds . . .'

'And they are . . . ?'

'Fighting monsters, defeating tyrants, stealing rare treasures, rescuing maidens . . . that sort of thing,' said Mr Betteridge vaguely. 'You know . . . heroic things.'

'And who, precisely, defines the monstrousness of the monsters and the tyranny of the tyrants?' said Lord Vetinari, his voice suddenly like a scalpel – not vicious like a sword, but probing its edge into vulnerable places.

Mr Betteridge shifted uneasily. 'Well . . . the hero, I suppose.'

'Ah. And the theft of these rare items . . . I think the word that interests me here is the term "theft", an activity frowned on by most of the world's major religions, is it not? The feeling stealing over me is that *all* these terms are defined by the hero. You could say: I am a hero, so when I kill you that makes you, *de facto*, the kind of person suitable to be killed by a hero. You could say that a hero, in short, is someone who indulges every whim that, within the rule of law, would have him behind bars or swiftly dancing what I believe is known as the hemp fandango. The words *we* might use are: murder, pillage, theft and rape. Have I understood the situation?'

'Not rape, I believe,' said Mr Betteridge, finding a rock on which he could stand. 'Not in the case of Cohen the Barbarian. Ravishing, possibly.'

'There is a difference?'

'It's more a matter of approach, I understand,' said the historian. 'I don't believe there were ever any actual complaints.'

'Speaking as a lawyer,' said Mr Slant of the Guild of Lawyers, 'it is clear that the first ever recorded heroic deed to which the message refers was an act of theft from the rightful owners. The legends of many different cultures testify to this.'

'Was it something you could actually *steal*?' said Ridcully.

'Manifestly *yes*,' said the lawyer. 'Theft is central to the legend. Fire was *stolen* from the gods.'

'This is not currently the issue,' said Lord Vetinari. 'The issue, gentlemen, is that Cohen the Barbarian is climbing the mountain on which the gods live. And we cannot stop him. And he intends to *return* fire to the gods. Fire, in this case, in the shape of . . . let me see—'

Ponder Stibbons looked up from his notebooks, where he had been scribbling.

'A fifty-pound keg of Agatean Thunder Clay,' he said. 'I'm amazed their wizards let him have it.'

'He was . . . indeed, I assume he still *is* the Emperor,' said Lord Vetinari. 'So I would imagine that when the supreme ruler of your continent asks you for something, it is not the time for a prudent man to ask for a docket signed by Mr Jenkins of Requisitions.'

'Thunder Clay is terribly powerful stuff,' said Ridcully. 'But it needs a special detonator. You have to smash a jar of acid inside the mixture. The acid soaks into it, and then – kablooie, I believe the term is.'

'Unfortunately the prudent man also saw fit to give one of these to Cohen,' said Lord Vetinari. 'And if the resulting kablooie takes place atop the mountain, which is the hub of the world's magic field, it will, as I understand it, result in the field collapsing for . . . remind me, Mister Stibbons?'

'About two years,' he said.

'Really? Well, we can do without magic for a couple of years, can't we?' said Mr Slant, managing to suggest that this would be a jolly good thing too.

'With respect,' said Ponder, without respect, 'we cannot. The seas will run dry. The sun will burn out and crash. The elephants and the turtle may cease to exist altogether.'

'That'll happen in just two years?'

'Oh, no. That'll happen within a few minutes, sir. You see, magic isn't just coloured lights and balls. Magic holds the world together.'

In the sudden silence, Lord Vetinari's voice sounded crisp and clear.

'Is there anyone who knows *anything* about Ghengiz Cohen?' he said. 'And is there *anyone* who can tell us why, before leaving the city, he and his men kidnapped a harmless minstrel from our embassy? Explosives, *yes*, very barbaric . . . but why a minstrel? Can anyone tell me?'

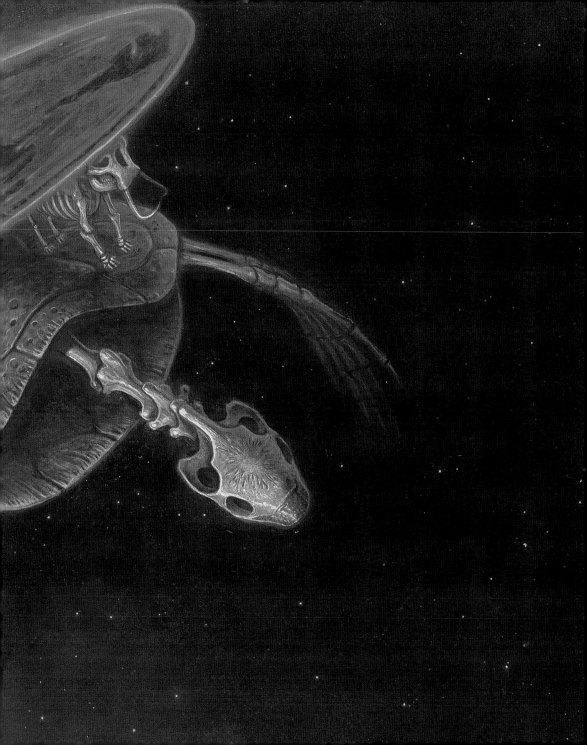

Truckle
the Uncivil

here was a bitter wind this close to Cori Celesti. From here the world mountain, which looked like a needle from afar, was a raw and ragged cascade of ascending peaks. The central spire was lost in a haze of snow crystals, miles high. The sun sparkled on them. Several elderly men sat huddled around a fire.

'I hope he's right about the stair of light,' said Boy Willie. 'We're going to look real muffins if it isn't there.'

'He was right about the giant walrus,' said Truckle the Uncivil.

'When?'

'Remember when we were crossing the ice? When he shouted, "Look out! We're going to be attacked by a giant walrus!"'

'Oh, yeah.'

Willie looked back up at the spire. The air seemed thinner already, the colours deeper, making him feel that he could reach up and touch the sky. 'Anyone know if there's a lavatory at the top?' he said.

'Oh, there's *got* to be,' said Caleb the Ripper. 'Yeah, I'm sure I heard tell about it. The Toilet of the Gods.'

'Whut?'

They turned to what appeared to be a pile of furs on wheels. When the eye knew what it was looking for this became an ancient wheelchair, mounted on skis and covered with rags of blanket and animal skins. A pair of beady, animal eyes peered out suspiciously from the heap. There was a barrel strapped behind the wheelchair.

'It must be time for his gruel,' said Boy Willie, putting a soot-encrusted pot on the fire.

'Whut?'

'JUST WARMING UP YOUR GRUEL, HAMISH!'

'Bludy walrus again?'

'YES!'

'Whut?'

They were, all of them, old men. Their background conversation was a litany of complaints about feet, stomachs and backs. They moved slowly. But they had a *look* about them. It was in their eyes.

Their eyes said that, wherever it was, they had been there. Whatever it was, they had done it, sometimes more than once. But they would never, ever, *buy* the T-shirt. And they *did* know the meaning of the word 'fear'. It was something that happened to other people.

'I wish Old Vincent was here,' said Caleb the Ripper, poking the fire aimlessly.

'Well, he's gone, and there's an end of it,' said Truckle the Uncivil, shortly. 'We said we weren't going to bloody talk about it.'

'But what a way to go . . . gods, I hope that doesn't happen to me. Something like *that* . . . it shouldn't happen to anyone—'

'Yes, all right,' said Truckle.

Boy Willie

25

'He was a good bloke. Took everything the world threw at him.'

'*All right.*'

'And then to choke on—'

'We all know! Now bloody well shut up!'

'Dinner's done,' said Caleb, pulling a smoking slab of grease out of the embers. 'Nice walrus steak, anyone? What about Mr Pretty?'

They turned to an evidently human figure that had been propped against a boulder. It was indistinct, because of the ropes, but it was clearly dressed in brightly coloured clothes. This wasn't the place for brightly coloured clothes. This was a land for fur and leather.

Boy Willie walked over to the colourful thing.

'We'll take the gag off,' he said, 'if you promise not to scream.'

Frantic eyes darted this way and that, and then the gagged head nodded.

'All right, then. Eat your your nice walrus . . . er, lump,' said Boy Willie, pulling at the cloth.

'How *dare* you drag me all—' the minstrel began.

'Now *look*,' said Boy Willie, 'none of us like havin' to wallop you alongside the ear when you go on like this, do we? Be reasonable.'

'*Reasonable*? When you kidnap—'

Boy Willie snapped the gag back into place.

'Thin streak of nothin',' he muttered at the angry eyes. 'You ain't even got a harp. What kind of bard doesn't even have a harp? Just this sort of little wooden pot thing. Damn silly idea.'

''s called a lute,' said Caleb, through a mouthful of walrus.

'Whut?'

'IT'S CALLED A LUTE, HAMISH!'

'Aye, I used to loot!'

'Nah, it's for singin' posh songs for ladies,' said Caleb. 'About . . . flowers and that. *Romance.*'

The Horde knew the word, although the activity had been outside the scope of their busy lives.

'Amazin', what songs do for the ladies,' said Caleb.

'Well, when *I* was a lad,' said Truckle, 'if you wanted to get a girl's int'rest, you had to cut off your worst enemy's wossname and present it to her.'

'Whut?'

'I SAID YOU HAD TO CUT OFF YOUR WORST ENEMY'S WOSSNAME AND PRESENT IT TO HER!'

'Aye, romance is a wonderful thing,' said Mad Hamish.

'What'd you do if you didn't have a worst enemy?' said Boy Willie.

'You try and cut off anyone's wossname,' said Truckle, 'and you've soon got a worst enemy.'

'Flowers is more usual these days,' said Caleb, reflectively.

Truckle eyed the struggling lutist.

'Can't think what the boss was thinking of, draggin' this thing along,' he said. 'Where is he, anyway?'

Mad
Hamish

27

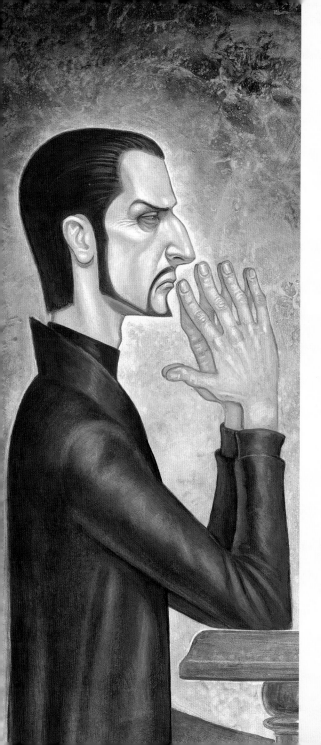

ord Vetinari, despite his education, had a mind like an engineer. If you wished to open something, you found the appropriate spot and applied the minimum amount of force necessary to achieve your end. Possibly the spot was between a couple of ribs and the force was applied via a dagger, or between two warring countries and applied via an army, but the important thing was to find that one weak spot which would be the key to everything.

'And so you are now the unpaid Professor of Cruel and Unusual Geography?' he said to the figure who had been brought before him.

The wizard known as Rincewind nodded slowly, just in case an admission was going to get him into trouble.

'Er . . . yes?'

'Have you been to the Hub?'

'Er . . . yes?'

'Can you describe the terrain?'

'Er . . . '

'What did the scenery look like?' Lord Vetinari added helpfully.

'Er . . . blurred, sir. I was being chased by some people.'

'Indeed? And why was this?'

Rincewind looked shocked. 'Oh, I *never* stop to find out why people are chasing me, sir. I never look behind, either. That'd be rather silly, sir.'

Lord Vetinari pinched the bridge of his nose. 'Just tell me what you know about Cohen, please,' he said wearily.

'Him? He's just a hero who never died, sir. A leathery old man. Not very bright, really, but he's got so much cunning and guile you'd never know it.'

'Are you a friend of his?'

'Well, we've met a couple of times and he didn't kill me,' said Rincewind. 'That probably counts as a "yes".'

'And what about the old men who're with him?'

'Oh, they're not old men . . . well, yes, they *are* old men . . . but, well . . . they're his Silver Horde, sir.'

'*Those* are the Silver Horde? *All* of it?'

'Yes, sir,' said Rincewind.

'But I thought the Silver Horde conquered the entire Agatean Empire!'

'Yes, sir. That was them.' Rincewind shook his head. 'I know it's hard to believe, sir. But you haven't seen them fight. They're *experienced*. And the thing is . . . the *big* thing about Cohen is . . . he's contagious.'

'You mean he's a plague carrier?'

'It's like a mental illness, sir. Or magic. He's as crazy as a stoat, but . . . once they've been around him for a while, people start seeing the world the way he does. All big and simple. And they want to be part of it.'

Lord Vetinari looked at his fingernails. 'But I understood that these men had settled down and were immensely rich and powerful,' he said. 'That's what heroes want, isn't it? To crush the thrones of the world beneath their sandalled feet, as the poet puts it?'

'Yes, sir.'

'So what's this? One last throw of the dice? *Why?*'

'I can't understand it, sir. I mean . . . they had it all.'

'Clearly,' said the Patrician. 'But everything wasn't enough, was it?'

here was argument in the anteroom beyond the Patrician's Oblong Office. Every few minutes a clerk slipped in through a side door and laid another pile of papers on the desk.

Lord Vetinari stared at them. Possibly, he felt, the thing to do would be to wait until the pile of international advice and demands grew as tall as Cori Celesti, and simply climb to the top of it.

Zip, zing and can-do, he thought.

So, as a man full of get up and go must do, Lord Vetinari got up and went. He unlocked a secret door in the panelling and a moment later was gliding silently through the hidden corridors of his palace.

The dungeons of the palace held a number of felons imprisoned 'at his lordship's pleasure', and since Lord Vetinari was seldom very pleased they were generally in for the long haul. His destination now, though, was the strangest prisoner of all, who lived in the attic.

Leonard of Quirm had never committed a crime. He regarded his fellow man with benign interest. He was an artist and he was also the cleverest man alive, if you used the word 'clever' in a specialised and technical sense. But Lord Vetinari felt that the world was not yet ready for a man who designed unthinkable weapons of war as a happy hobby. The man was, in his heart and soul, *and in everything he did*, an artist.

Currently, Leonard was painting a picture of a lady from a series of sketches he had pinned up by his easel.

'Ah, my lord,' he said, glancing up. 'And what is the problem?'

'Is there a problem?' said Lord Vetinari.

'There generally is, my lord, when you come to see me.'

'Very well,' said Lord Vetinari. 'I wish to get several people to the centre of the world as soon as possible.'

'Ah, yes,' said Leonard. 'There is much treacherous terrain between here and there. Do you think I have the smile right? I've never been very good at smiles.'

'I *said*—'

'Do you wish them to arrive alive?'

'What? Oh . . . yes. Of course. And *fast*.'

Leonard painted on, in silence. Lord Vetinari knew better than to interrupt.

'And do you wish them to return?' said the artist, after a while. 'You know, perhaps I should show the teeth. I believe I understand teeth.'

'Returning them would be a pleasant bonus, yes.'

'This is a vital journey?'

'If it is not successful, the world will end.'

'Ah. Quite vital, then.' Leonard laid down his brush and stood back, looking critically at his picture. 'I shall require the use of several sailing ships and a large barge,' he said, after a while. 'And I will make a list of other materials for you.'

'A sea voyage?'

'To begin with, my lord.'

'Are you *sure* you don't want further time to think?' said Lord Vetinari.

'Oh, to sort out the fine detail, yes. But I believe I already have the essential idea.'

Vetinari looked up at the ceiling of the workroom and the armada of paper shapes and bat-winged devices and other aerial extravaganzas that hung there, turning gently in the breeze.

'This doesn't involve some kind of flying machine, does it?' he said suspiciously.

'Um . . . why do you ask?'

'Because the destination is a very high place, Leonard, and your flying machines have an inevitable *downwards* component.'

'Yes, my lord. But I believe that sufficient *down* eventually becomes up, my lord.'

'Ah. Is this philosophy?'

'*Practical* philosophy, my lord.'

'Nevertheless, I find myself amazed, Leonard, that you appear to have come up with a solution just as soon as I presented the problem . . .'

Leonard of Quirm cleaned his brush. 'I always say, my lord, that a problem correctly posed contains its own solution. But it is true to say that I have given some thought to issues of this nature. I do, as you know, *experiment* with devices . . . which of course, obedient to your views on this matter, I subsequently dismantle because there are indeed evil men in the world who might stumble upon them and pervert their use. You were kind enough to give me a room with unlimited views of the sky, and I . . . notice things. Oh . . . I shall require several dozen swamp dragons, too. No, that should be . . . more than a hundred, I think.'

'Ah, you intend to build a ship that can be drawn into the sky by dragons?' said Lord Vetinari, mildly relieved. 'I recall an old story about a ship that was pulled by swans and flew all the way to—'

'Swans, I fear, would not work. But your surmise is broadly correct, my lord. Well done. *Two* hundred dragons, I suggest, to be on the safe side.'

'That at least is not a difficulty. They are becoming rather a pest.'

'And the help of, oh, sixty apprentices and journeymen from the Guild of Cunning Artificers. Perhaps there should be a hundred. They will need to work round the clock.'

'Apprentices? But I can see to it that the finest craftsmen—'

Leonard held up a hand.

'Not craftsmen, my lord,' he said. 'I have no use for people who have learned the limits of the possible.'

p on the mountain, as the blizzards closed in, there was a red glow in the snow. It was there all winter, and when the spring gales blew, the rubies glittered in the sunshine.

No one remembers the singer. The song remains.

The Horde found Cohen sitting on an ancient burial mound a little way from the camp.
There were a lot of them in this area. The members of the Horde had seen them
before sometimes, on their various travels across the world. Here and there an
ancient stone would poke through the snow, carved in a language none of them
recognised. They were very old. None of the Horde had ever considered cutting into a mound
to see what treasures might lie within. Partly this was because they had a word for people who
used shovels, and that word was 'slave'. But mainly it was because, despite their calling, they
had a keen moral Code, even if it wasn't the sort adopted by nearly everyone else, and this
Code led them to have a word for anyone who disturbed a burial mound. That word was 'Die!'.

The Horde, each member a veteran of a thousand hopeless charges, nevertheless advanced
cautiously towards Cohen, who was sitting cross-legged in the snow. His sword was thrust
deep into a drift. He had a distant, worrying expression.

'Coming to have some dinner, old friend?' said Caleb.

'It's *walrus*,' said Boy Willie. 'Again.'

Cohen grunted.

'I havfen't finiffed,' he said, indistinctly.

'Finished what, old friend?'

'Rememb'rin',' said Cohen.

'Remembering who?'

'The hero who waff buried here, all right?'

'Who was he?'

'Dunno.'

'Who were his people?'

'Fearch me,' said Cohen.

'Did he do any mighty deeds?'

'Couldn't fay.'

'Then *why*—?'

'*Fomeone'f* got to remember the poor bugger!'

'You don't know anything about him!'

'I can ftill *remember* him!'

The rest of the Horde exchanged glances. This was going to be a difficult adventure. It was a good job that it was to be the last.

'You ought to come and have a word with that bard we captured,' said Caleb. 'He's getting on my nerves. He don't seem to understand what he's about.'

'He'f juft got to write the faga afterwardf,' said Cohen flatly and damply. A thought appeared to strike him. He started to pat various parts of his clothing, which, given the amount of clothing, didn't take long.

'Yeah, well, this isn't your basic heroic saga kind of bard, y'see,' said Caleb, as his leader continued the search. 'I *told* you he wasn't the right sort when we grabbed him. He's more the kind of bard you want if you need some ditty being sung to a girl. We're talking flowers and spring here, boss.'

'Ah, got 'em,' said Cohen. From a bag on his belt he produced a set of dentures, carved from the diamond teeth of trolls. He inserted them in his mouth and gnashed them a few times. 'That's better. What were you saying?'

'He's not a proper bard, boss.'

Cohen shrugged. 'He'll just have to learn fast, then. He's got to be better'n the ones back in the Empire. They don't have a clue about poems longer'n seventeen syllables. At least this one's from Ankh-Morpork. He must've *heard* about sagas.'

'I *said* we should've stopped off at Whale Bay,' said Truckle. 'Icy wastes, freezing nights . . . good saga country.'

'Yeah, if you like blubber.' Cohen drew his sword from the snowdrift. 'I reckon I'd better go and take the lad's mind off of flowers, then.'

'It appears that things revolve around the Disc,' said Leonard. 'This is certainly the case with the sun and the moon. And also, if you recall . . . the *Maria Pesto*?'

'The ship they said went right under the Disc?' said Archchancellor Ridcully.

'Quite. Known to be blown over the Rim near the Bay of Mante during a dreadful storm, and seen by fishermen rising above the Rim near TinLing some days later, where it crashed down upon a reef. There was only one survivor, whose dying words were . . . rather strange.'

'I remember,' said Ridcully. 'He said, "My God, it's full of elephants!"'

'It is my view that with sufficient thrust and a lateral component a craft sent off the edge of the world would be swung underneath by the massive attraction and rise on the far side,' said Leonard, 'probably to a sufficient height to allow it to glide down to anywhere on the surface.'

The wizards stared at the blackboard. Then, as one wizard, they turned to Ponder Stibbons, who was scribbling in his notebook.

'What was that about, Ponder?'

Ponder stared at his notes. Then he stared at Leonard. Then he stared at Ridcully.

'Er . . . yes. Possibly. Er . . . if you fall over the edge fast enough, the . . . world pulls you back . . . and you go on falling but it's all *round* the world.'

Cohen the
Barbarian

'You're saying that by falling off the world we – and by *we*, I hasten to point out, I don't actually include myself – we can end up in the *sky*?' said the Dean.

'Um . . . yes. After all, the sun does the same thing every day . . . '

The Dean looked enraptured. 'Amazing!' he said. 'Then . . . you could get an army into the heart of enemy territory! No fortress would be safe! You could rain fire down on to—'

He caught the look in Leonard's eye.

'—on to bad people,' he finished, lamely.

'That would *not* happen,' said Leonard severely. '*Ever!*'

'Could the . . . thing you are planning land on Cori Celesti?' said Lord Vetinari.

'Oh, certainly there should be suitable snowfields up there,' said Leonard. 'If there are not, I feel sure I can devise some appropriate landing method. Happily, as you have pointed out, things in the air have a tendency to come down.'

Ridcully was about to make an appropriate comment, but stopped himself. He knew Leonard's reputation. This was a man who could invent seven new things before breakfast, including two new ways with toast. This man had invented the ball-bearing, such an obvious device that no one had thought of it. That was the very centre of his genius – he invented things that anyone could have thought of, and men who can invent things that anyone could have thought of are very rare men.

This man was so absentmindedly clever that he could paint pictures that didn't just follow you around the room but went home with you and did the washing-up.

Some people are confident because they are fools. Leonard had the look of someone who was confident because, so far, he'd never found a reason not to be. He would step off a high building in the happy state of mind of someone who intended to deal with the problem of the ground when it presented itself.

And might.

'What do you need from us?' said Ridcully.

'Well, the . . . thing cannot operate by magic. Magic will be unreliable near the Hub, I understand. But can you supply me with wind?'

'You have certainly chosen the right people,' said Lord Vetinari. And it seemed to the wizards that there was just too long a pause before he went on, 'They are highly skilled in weather manipulation.'

'A severe gale would be helpful at the launch . . . ' Leonard continued.

'I think I can say without fear of contradiction that our wizards can supply wind in practically unlimited amounts,' said the Patrician. 'Is that not so, Archchancellor?'

'I am *forced* to agree, my lord.'

'Then if we can rely on a stiff following breeze, I am sure—'

'Just a moment, just a moment,' said the Dean, who rather felt the wind comment had been directed at him. 'What do we know of this man? He makes . . . devices, and paints pictures, does he? Well, I'm sure this is all very nice, but we all know about artists, don't we? Flibbertigibbets, to a man. And what about Bloody Stupid Johnson? Remember some of the

things *he* built?* I'm sure Mr da Quirm draws lovely pictures, but I for one would need a *little* more evidence of his amazing genius before we entrust the world to his . . . device. Show me one thing he can do that anyone couldn't do, if they had the time.'

'I have never considered myself a genius,' said Leonard, looking down bashfully and doodling on the paper in front of him.

'Well, if *I* was a genius I think I'd know it—' the Dean began, and stopped.

Absentmindedly, while barely paying attention to what he was doing, Leonard had drawn a perfect circle.

Lord Vetinari found it best to set up a committee system. More of the ambassadors from other countries had arrived at the university, and more heads of the Guilds were pouring in, and every single one of them wanted to be involved in the decision-making process, without necessarily going through the intelligence-using process first.

About seven committees, he considered, should be about right. And when, ten minutes later, the first sub-committee had miraculously budded off, he took aside a few chosen people into a small room, set up the Miscellaneous Committee, and locked the door.

'The flying ship will need a crew, I'm told,' he said. 'It can carry three people. Leonard will have to go because, to be frank, he will be working on it even as it departs. And the other two?'

'There should be an assassin,' said Lord Downey of the Assassins' Guild.

'No. If Cohen and his friends were easy to assassinate, they would have been dead long ago,' said Lord Vetinari.

'Perhaps a woman's touch?' said Mrs Palm, head of the Guild of Seamstresses. 'I know they are elderly gentlemen, but my members are—'

'I think the problem there, Mrs Palm, is that although the Horde are apparently very appreciative of the company of women, they don't listen to anything they say. Yes, Captain Carrot?'

Captain Carrot Ironfoundersson of the City Watch was standing to attention, radiating keenness and a hint of soap.

'I volunteer to go, sir,' he said.

'Yes, I thought you probably would.'

'Is this a *matter* for the Watch?' said the lawyer Mr Slant. 'Mr Cohen is simply returning property to its original owner.'

'That is an insight which had not hitherto occurred to me,' said Lord Vetinari smoothly. 'However, the City Watch would not be the men I think they are if they couldn't think of a reason to arrest *anyone*. Commander Vimes?'

'Conspiracy to make an affray should do it,' said the head of the Watch, lighting a cigar.

'And Captain Carrot is a persuasive young man,' said Lord Vetinari.

'With a big sword,' grumbled Mr Slant.

*Many of the things built by the architect and freelance designer Bergholt Stuttley ('Bloody Stupid') Johnson were recorded in Ankh-Morpork, often on the line where it says 'Cause of Death'. He was, people agreed, a genius, at least if you defined the word broadly. Certainly no one else in the world could make an explosive mixture out of common sand and water. A good designer, he always said, should be capable of anything. And, indeed, he was.

'Persuasion comes in many forms,' said Lord Vetinari. 'No, I agree with Archchancellor Ridcully, sending Captain Carrot would be an excellent idea.'

'What? Did I say something?' said Ridcully.

'Do you think that sending Captain Carrot would be an excellent idea?'

'What? Oh. Yes. Good lad. Keen. Got a sword.'

'Then I agree with you,' said Lord Vetinari, who knew how to work a committee. 'We must make haste, gentlemen. The flotilla needs to leave tomorrow. We need a third member of the crew—'

There was a knock at the door. Vetinari signalled to a college porter to open it.

The wizard known as Rincewind lurched into the room, white-faced, and stopped in front of the table.

'I do not wish to volunteer for this mission,' he said.

'I beg your pardon?' said Lord Vetinari.

'I do not wish to volunteer, sir.'

'No one was asking you to.'

Rincewind wagged a weary finger. 'Oh, but they will, sir, they will. Someone will say: hey, that Rincewind fella, he's the adventurous sort, he *knows* the Horde, Cohen seems to like him, he knows all there is to know about cruel and unusual geography, he'd be just the job for something like this.' He sighed. 'And then I'll run away, and probably hide in a crate somewhere that'll be loaded on to the flying machine in any case.'

'Will you?'

'Probably, sir. Or there'll be a whole string of accidents that end up causing the same thing. Trust me, sir. I know how my life works. So I thought I'd better cut through the whole tedious business and come along and tell you I don't wish to volunteer.'

'I think you've left out a logical step somewhere,' said the Patrician.

'No, sir. It's very simple. I'm volunteering. I just don't *wish* to. But, after all, when did that ever have anything to do with anything?'

'He's got a point, you know,' said Ridcully. 'He seems to come back from all sorts of—'

'You see?' Rincewind gave Lord Vetinari a jaded smile. 'I've been living my life for a long time. I know how it works.'

Vena the
Raven-Haired

here were always robbers near the Hub. There were pickings to be had among the lost valleys and forbidden temples, and also among the less prepared adventurers. Too many people, when listing all the perils to be found in the search for lost treasure or ancient wisdom, had forgotten to put at the top of the list 'the man who arrived just before you'.

One such party was patrolling its favourite area when it espied, first, a well-equipped warhorse tethered to a frost-shrivelled tree. Then it saw a fire, burning in a small hollow out of the wind, with a small pot bubbling beside it. Finally it saw the woman. She was attractive, or, at least, had been conventionally so perhaps thirty years ago. Now she looked like the teacher you wished you'd had in your first year at school, the one with the understanding approach to life's little accidents, such as a shoe full of wee.

She had a blanket around her to keep out the cold. She was knitting. Stuck in the snow beside her was the largest sword the robbers had ever seen.

Intelligent robbers would have started to count up the incongruities here.

These, however, were the other kind, the kind for whom evolution was *invented*.

The woman glanced up, nodded at them, and went on with her knitting.

'Well now, what have we here?' said the leader. 'Are you—'

'Hold this, will you?' said the old woman, standing up. 'Over your thumbs, young man. It won't take a moment for me to wind a fresh ball. I was hoping someone would drop by.'

She held out a skein of wool.

The robber took it uncertainly, aware of the grins on the faces of his men. But he opened his arms with what he hoped was a suitably evil little-does-she-suspect look on his face.

'That's right,' said the old woman, standing back. She kicked him viciously in the groin in an incredibly efficient if unladylike way, reached down as he toppled, caught up the cauldron, flung it accurately at the face of the first henchman, and picked up her knitting before *he* fell.

The two surviving robbers hadn't had time to move, but then one unfroze and leapt for the sword. He staggered back under its weight, but the blade was long and reassuring.

'Aha!' he said, and grunted as he raised the sword. 'How the hell did you carry this, old woman?'

'It's not my sword,' she said. 'It belonged to the man over there.'

The man risked a look sideways. A pair of feet in armoured sandals were just visible behind a rock. They were very big feet.

But I've got a weapon, he thought. And then he thought: *so did he.*

The old woman sighed and drew two knitting needles from the ball of wool. The light glinted on them, and the blanket slid away from her shoulders and fell on to the snow.

'Well, gentlemen?' she said.

Cohen pulled the gag off the minstrel's mouth. The man stared at him in terror.

'What's your name, son?' said Cohen.

'You kidnapped me! I was walking along the street and—'

'How much?' said Cohen.

'What?'

'How much to write me a saga?'

'You *stink*!'

'Yeah, it's the walrus,' said Cohen evenly. 'It's a bit like garlic in that respect. Anyway . . . a saga, that's what I want. And what you want is a big bag of rubies, not unadjacent in size to the rubies what I have here.'

He upended a leather bag into the palm of his hand. The stones were so big the snow glowed red. The musician stared at them.

'You got – what's that word, Truckle?' said Cohen.

'Art,' said Truckle.

'You got art, and we got rubies. We give you rubies, you give us art,' said Cohen. 'End of problem, right?'

'Problem?' The rubies were hypnotic.

'Well, mainly the problem you'll have if you tell me you can't write me a saga,' said Cohen, still in a pleasant tone of voice.

'But . . . look, I'm sorry, but . . . sagas are just primitive poems, aren't they?'

The wind, never ceasing here near the Hub, had several seconds in which to produce its more forlorn yet threatening whistle.

'It'll be a long walk to *civilisation*, all by yourself,' said Truckle, at length.

'Without yer feet,' said Boy Willie.

'Please!'

'Nah, nah, lads, we don't want to do that to the boy,' said Cohen. 'He's a bright lad, got a great future ahead of him . . .' He took a pull of his home-rolled cigarette and added, 'up until now. Nah, I can see he's thinking about it. A heroic saga, lad. It'll be the most famousest one ever.'

'What about?'

'Us.'

'You? But you're all ol—'

The minstrel stopped. Even after a life that had hitherto held no danger greater than a

hurled meat bone at a banquet, he could recognise sudden death when he saw it. And he saw it now. Age hadn't weakened here – well, except in one or two places. Mostly, it had hardened.

'I wouldn't know how to compose a saga,' he said feebly.

'We'll help,' said Truckle.

'We know *lots*,' said Boy Willie.

'Been in most of 'em,' said Cohen.

The minstrel's thoughts ran like this: These men are *rubies* insane. They are *rubies* sure to kill me. *Rubies*. They've dragged me *rubies* all the *rubies rubies*.

They want to give me a big bag of *rubies* rubies . . .

'I suppose I could extend my repertoire,' he mumbled. A look at their faces made him readjust his vocabulary. 'All right, I'll do it,' he said. A tiny bit of honesty, though, survived even the glow of the jewels. 'I'm not the world's *greatest* minstrel, you know.'

'You will be after you write this saga,' said Cohen, untying his ropes.

'Well . . . I hope you like it . . . '

Cohen grinned again. ''S'not up to *us* to like it. We won't hear it,' he said.

'What? But you just said you wanted me to write you a saga—'

'Yeah, yeah. But it's gonna be the saga of how we died.'

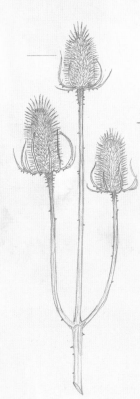

Common or fuller's Teasel,
as used in my gig-mill invention to raise
the nap of woollen cloth.
 Note burrs.

Pan

 Exercise: achieve adhesion in Weightless Air. Extruded Wire Loops may be of help, thus
creating 'stickyness' to any Rough Surface. May have limited use as clothes fastenings, etc?
So much world, so little time...

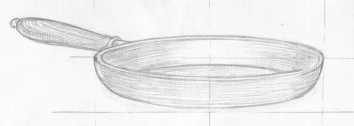

It appears to me that the substance that surrounds our world is as navigable
as the sea or the air, having instead of winds and currents the shaping of the
ether by the presence of matter in greater or lesser amounts. The sun and moon
and the minor planets, which I believe are made of elephant dung, daily
circumnavigate the Turtle by a process which I may describe as 'a fall which
never ends', or ringpath. All is a matter of thrust and direction and curves that
may be described with absolute accuracy. In the world, imperfection; in the
heavens, the sublime geometry.

It was a small flotilla that set sail from Ankh-Morpork next day. Things had happened quickly. It wasn't that the prospect of the end of the world was concentrating minds unduly, because that is a general and universal danger that people find hard to imagine. But the Patrician was being rather sharp with people, and that is a specific and highly personal danger and people had no problem relating to it at all.

The barge, under whose huge tarpaulin something was already taking shape, wallowed between the boats. Lord Vetinari went aboard only once, and looked gloomily at the vast piles of material that littered the deck.

'This is costing us a considerable amount of money,' he told Leonard, who had set up an easel. 'I just hope there will be something to show for it.'

'The continuation of the species, perhaps,' said Leonard, completing a complex drawing and handing it to an apprentice.

'Obviously *that*, yes.'

'We shall learn many new things,' said Leonard, 'that I am sure will be of immense benefit to posterity. For example, the survivor of the *Maria Pesto* reported that things floated around in the air as if they had become extremely light, so I have devised *this*.'

He reached down and picked up what looked, to Lord Vetinari, like a perfectly normal kitchen utensil.

'It's a frying pan that sticks to anything,' he said, proudly. 'I got the idea from observing a type of teazel, which—'

'And this will be useful?' said Lord Vetinari.

'Oh, indeed. We will need to eat meals and cannot have hot fat floating around. The small details matter, my lord. I have also devised a pen which writes upside down.'

'Oh. Could you not simply turn the paper up the other way?'

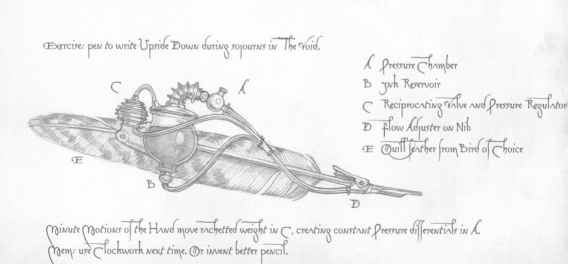

Exercise: pen to write Upside Down during sojourns in The Void.

A Pressure Chamber
B Ink Reservoir
C Reciprocating Valve and Pressure Regulator
D Flow Adjuster on Nib
E Quill feather from Bird of Choice

Minute Motions of the Hand move ratchetted weight in C, creating constant Pressure differentials in A. Mem: use Clockwork next time. Or invent better pencil.

The line of sledges moved across the snow.

'It's damn cold,' said Caleb.

'Feeling your age, are you?' said Boy Willie.

'You're as old as you feel, I always say.'

'Whut?'

'HE SAYS YOU'RE AS OLD AS YOU FEEL, HAMISH!'

'Whut? Feelin' whut?'

'I don't think I've become *old*,' said Boy Willie. 'Not your actual *old*. Just more aware of where the next lavatory is.'

'The worst bit,' said Truckle, 'is when young people come and sing happy songs at you.'

'Why're they so happy?' said Caleb.

''Cos they're not you, I suppose.'

Fine, sharp snow crystals, blown off the mountain tops, hissed across their vision. In deference to their profession, the Horde mostly wore tiny leather loincloths and bits and pieces of fur and chainmail. In deference to their advancing years, and entirely without comment among themselves, these had been underpinned now with long woolly combinations and various strange elasticated things. They were dealing with Time as they had dealt with nearly everything else in their lives, as something you charged at and tried to kill.

At the front of the party, Cohen was giving the minstrel some tips.

'First off, you got to describe how you *feel* about the saga,' he said. 'How singing it makes your blood race and you can hardly contain yourself . . . you got to tell 'em what a great saga it's gonna be . . . understand?'

'Yes, yes . . . I think so . . . and then I say who you are . . . ' said the minstrel, scribbling furiously.

'Nah, *then* you say what the weather was like.'

'You mean like, "It was a bright day"?'

'Nah, nah, *nah*. You got to talk *saga*. So, first off, you gotta put the sentences the wrong way round.'

'You mean like, "Bright was the day"?'

'Right! Good! I *knew* you was clever.'

'Clever you was, you mean!' said the minstrel, before he could stop himself.

46

There was a moment of heart-stopping uncertainty, and then Cohen grinned and slapped him on the back. It was like being hit with a shovel.

'That's the style! What else now . . . ? Ah, yes . . . no one ever talks, in sagas. They always spakes.'

'Spakes?'

'Like "Up spake Wulf the Sea-rover", see? An' . . . an' . . . an' people are always *the* something. Like me, I'm Cohen the Barbarian, right? But it could be "Cohen the Bold-hearted" or "Cohen the Slayer of Many", or any of that class of a thing.'

'Er . . . why are you doing this?' said the minstrel. 'I ought to put that in. You're going to *return* fire to the gods?'

'Yeah. With *interest*.'

'But . . . *why*?'

''Cos we've seen a lot of old friends die,' said Caleb.

'That's right,' said Boy Willie. 'And *we* never saw no big wimmin on flying horses come and take 'em to the Halls of Heroes.'

'When Old Vincent died, him being one of us,' said Boy Willie, 'where was the Bridge of Frost to take him to the Feast of the Gods, eh? No, they got him, they let him get soft with comfy beds and someone to chew his food for him. They nearly got us all.'

'Hah! Milky drinks!' spat Truckle.

'Whut?' said Hamish, waking up.

'HE ASKED WHY WE WANT TO RETURN FIRE TO THE GODS, HAMISH!'

'Eh? Someone's got to do it!' cackled Hamish.

'Because it's a big world and we ain't seen it all,' said Boy Willie.

'Because the buggers are immortal,' said Caleb.

'Because of the way my back aches on chilly nights,' said Truckle.

The minstrel looked at Cohen, who was staring at the ground.

'Because . . . ' said Cohen, 'because . . . they've let us grow old.'

At which point, the ambush was sprung. Snowdrifts erupted. Huge figures raced towards the Horde. Swords were in skinny, spotted hands with the speed born of experience. Clubs were swung—

'Hold everything!' shouted Cohen. It was a voice of command.

The fighters froze. Blades trembled an inch away from throat and torso.

Cohen looked up into the cracked and craggy features of an enormous troll, its club raised to smash him.

'Don't I *know* you?' he said.

he wizards were working in relays. Ahead of the fleet, an area of sea was mill-pond calm. From behind came a steady, unwavering breeze. The wizards *were* good at wind, weather being a matter not of force but of lepidoptery. As Archchancellor Ridcully said, you just had to know where the damn butterflies were.

And therefore some million-to-one chance must have sent the sodden log under the barge. The shock was slight, but Ponder Stibbons, who had been carefully rolling the omniscope across the deck, ended up on his back surrounded by twinkling shards.

Archchancellor Ridcully hurried across the deck, his voice full of concern.

'Is it badly damaged? That cost a hundred thousand dollars, Mr Stibbons! Oh, *look* at it! A dozen pieces!'

'I'm not badly hurt, Archchancellor—'

'Hundreds of hours of time *wasted*! And now we won't be able to watch the progress of the flight. Are you listening, Mr Stibbons?'

Ponder wasn't. He *was* holding two of the shards and staring at them.

'I think I may have stumbled, haha, on an amazing piece of serendipity, Archchancellor.'

'What say?'

'Has anyone ever broken an omniscope before, sir?'

'No, young man. And that is because other people are *careful* with expensive equipment!'

'Er . . . would you care to look in this piece, sir?' said Ponder urgently. 'I think it's very *important* you look at this piece, sir.'

p on the lower slopes of Cori Celesti, it was time for old times. Ambushers and ambushees had lit a fire.

'So how come you left the Evil Dark Lord business, Harry?' said Cohen.

'Werl, you know how it is these days,' said Evil Harry Dread.

The Horde nodded. They knew how it was these days.

'People these days, when they're attacking your Dark Evil Tower, the first thing they do is block up your escape tunnel,' said Evil Harry.

'Bastards!' said Cohen. 'You've *got* to let the Dark Lord escape. Everyone knows that.'

'That's right,' said Caleb. 'Got to leave yourself some work for tomorrow.'

'And it wasn't as if I didn't play fair,' said Evil Harry. 'I mean, I always left a secret back entrance to my Mountain of Dread, I employed really *stupid* people as cell guards—'

'Dat's me,' said the enormous troll proudly.

'—that was you, right, and I always made sure *all* my henchmen had the kind of helmets that covered the *whole* face, so an enterprising hero could disguise himself in one, and those come damn expensive, let me tell you.'

'Me and Evil Harry go *way* back,' said Cohen, rolling a cigarette. 'I knew him when he was starting up with just two lads and his Shed of Doom.'

'*And* Slasher, the Steed of Terror,' Evil Harry pointed out.

'Yes, but he was a donkey, Harry,' Cohen pointed out.

'He had a very nasty bite on him, though. He'd take your finger off as soon as look at you.'

'Didn't I fight you when you were the Doomed Spider God?' said Caleb.

'Probably. Everyone else did. They were great days,' said Harry. 'Giant spiders is always reliable, better'n octopussies, even.' He sighed. 'And then, of course, it all changed.'

They nodded. It *had* all changed.

'They *said* I was an evil stain covering the face of the world,' said Harry. 'Not a word about bringing jobs to areas of traditionally high unemployment. And then of course the big boys moved in, and you can't compete with an out-of-town site. Anyone heard of Ning the Uncompassionate?'

'Sort of,' said Boy Willie. 'I killed him.'

'You couldn't have done! What was it he always said? "I shall revert to this vicinity!"'

'Sort of hard to do that,' said Boy Willie, pulling out a pipe and beginning to fill it with tobacco, 'when your head's nailed to a tree.'

'How about Pamdar the Witch Queen?' said Evil Harry. 'Now *there* was—'

'Retired,' said Cohen.

'She'd never retire!'

EVIL HARRY DREAD

53

DAT'S ME

54

'Got married,' Cohen insisted. 'To Mad Hamish.'

'Whut?'

'I SAID YOU MARRIED PAMDAR, HAMISH,' Cohen shouted.

'Hehehehe, I did that! Whut?'

'That was some time ago, mark you,' said Boy Willie. 'I don't think it lasted.'

'But she was a devil woman!'

'We all get older, Harry. She runs a shop now. Pam's Pantry. Makes marmalade,' said Cohen.

'What? She used to queen it on a throne on top of a pile of skulls!'

'I didn't say it was very *good* marmalade.'

'How about you, Cohen?' said Evil Harry. 'I heard you were an Emperor.'

'Sounds good, doesn't it?' said Cohen mournfully. 'But you know what? It's dull. Everyone creepin' around bein' respectful, no one to fight, and those soft beds give you backache. All that money, and nothin' to spend it on 'cept toys. It sucks all the life right out of you, civilisation.'

'It killed Old Vincent the Ripper,' said Boy Willie. 'He choked to death on a concubine.'

There was no sound but the hiss of snow in the fire and a number of people thinking fast.

'I think you mean cucumber,' said the bard.

'That's right, cucumber,' said Boy Willie. 'I've never been good at them long words.'

'Very important difference in a salad situation,' said Cohen. He turned back to Evil Harry. 'That's no way for a hero to die, all soft and fat and eating big dinners. A hero should die in battle.'

'Yeah, but you lads've never got the hang of dying,' Evil Harry pointed out.

'That's because we haven't picked the right enemies,' said Cohen. 'This time we're going to see the gods.' He tapped the barrel he was sitting on, and the other members of the Horde winced when he did so. 'Got something here that belongs to them,' Cohen added.

SLIME

He glanced around the group and noted some almost imperceptible nods.

'Why don't you come with us, Evil Harry?' he said. 'You can bring your evil henchmen.'

Evil Harry drew himself up. 'Hey, I'm a Dark Lord! How'd it look if I was to go around with a bunch of heroes?'

'It wouldn't look *anything*,' said Cohen sharply. 'And I'll tell you for why, shall I? We're the last, see. Us 'n' you. No one else cares. There's no more heroes, Evil Harry. No more villains, neither.'

'Oh, there's always villains!' said Evil Harry.

'No, there's vicious evil underhand bastards, true enough. But they use laws now. They'd never call themselves Evil Harry.'

'Men who don't know the Code,' said Boy Willie. Everyone nodded. You mightn't live by the law but you had to live by the Code.

'Men with bits of paper,' said Caleb.

There was another group nod. The Horde were not great readers. Paper was the enemy, and so were the men who wielded it. Paper crept around you and took over the world.

'We always liked you, Harry,' said Cohen. 'You played it by the rules. How about it . . . are you coming with us?'

Evil Harry looked embarrassed. 'Well, I'd *like* to,' he said. 'But . . . well, I'm Evil Harry, right? You can't trust me an inch. First chance I get, I'll betray you all, stab you in the back or something . . .

BUTCHER

I'd *have* to, see? Of course, if it was up to *me*, it'd be different . . . but I've got a reputation to think about, right? I'm Evil Harry. Don't ask me to come.'

'Well spake,' said Cohen. 'I *like* a man I can't trust. You know where you stand with an untrustworthy man. It's the ones you ain't never sure about who give you grief. You come with us, Harry. You're one of us. And your lads, too. New ones, I see . . . ' Cohen raised his eyebrows.

'Well, yeah, you know how it is with the really *stupid* henchmen,' said Evil. 'This is Slime—'

' . . . nork nork,' said Slime.

'Ah, one of the old Stupid Lizard Men,' said Cohen. 'Good to see there's one left. Hey, two left. And this one is—?'

' . . . nork nork.'

'He's Slime, too,' said Evil Harry, patting the second lizard man gingerly to avoid the spikes. 'Never good at remembering more than one name, your basic Lizard Man. Over here we have . . . ' He nodded at something vaguely like a dwarf, who gave him an imploring look.

'You're Armpit,' prompted Evil Harry.

'Your Armpit,' said Armpit gratefully.

' . . . nork nork,' said one of the Slimes, in case this remark had been addressed to him.

'Well done, Harry,' said Cohen. 'It's damn hard to find a really stupid dwarf.'

'Wasn't easy, I can tell you,' Harry admitted proudly as he moved on. 'And this is Butcher.'

'Good name, good name,' said Cohen, looking up at the enormous fat man. 'Your jailer, right?'

'Took a lot of finding,' said Evil Harry, while Butcher grinned happily at nothing. 'Believes anything anyone tells him, can't see through the most ridiculous disguise, would let a transvestite washerwoman go free even if she had a beard you could camp in, falls asleep real easily on a chair near the bars and—'

'—carries his keys on a big hook on his belt so's they can be easily lifted off!' said Cohen. 'Classic. A master touch, that. And you've got a troll, I see.'

'Dat's me,' said the troll.

' . . . nork, nork.'

ARMPIT

GAK

(The obligatory skeletal henchman.)

58

'Dat's me.'

'Well, you've got to have a troll, haven't you?' said Evil Harry. 'Bit brighter than I'd like, but he's got no sense of direction and can't remember his name.'

'And what do we have here?' said Cohen. 'A real old zombie? Where did you dig him up? I like a man who's not afraid to let all his flesh fall off.'

'Gak,' said the zombie.

'No tongue, eh?' said Cohen. 'Don't worry, lad, a blood-curdling screech is all you need. And a few bits of wire, by the look of it. It's all a matter of style.'

'Dat's me.'

'. . . nork nork.'

'Gak.'

'Dat's me.'

'Your Armpit.'

'They must make you proud. I don't know when I've ever seen a more stupid bunch of henchmen,' said Cohen, admiring. 'Harry, you're like a refreshin' fart in a roomful of roses. You bring 'em all along. I wouldn't hear of you staying behind.'

'Nice to be appreciated,' said Evil Harry, looking down and blushing.

'And what else've you got to look forward to, anyway?' said Cohen. 'Who really *appreciates* a good Dark Lord these days? The world's too complicated now. It don't belong to the likes of us any more . . . it chokes us to death with cucumbers.'

'What are you actually going to *do*, Cohen?' said Evil Harry.

'. . . nork, nork.'

'Well, I reckon it's time to go out like we started,' said Cohen. 'One last roll of the dice.' He tapped the keg again. 'It's time,' he said, 'to give something back.'

'. . . nork, nork.'

'Shut up.'

SLIME

Varieties of the Swamp Dragon

1 The Smooth Courser. Note elongation of the feems.

2 Ramkin's Optimist. Good-natured, seldom explodes.

3 The Nothingfjord Blue. Wonderful scales, but a tendency to homesickness.

4 The Smooth-nosed Smut.

5 The Big-nosed Jolly. Frightened of shovels.

6 The Rough-nosed Smut (elderly male).

7 Wivelspiker. Excitable. Walks into windows.

8 The Quirmian Long-ear. Mild-natured, but needs daily exercise.

9 Spiked Oncer. Rare, needs much attention.

10 The Classic Smut. A very popular dragon in the traditional mould.

11 Golden Deceiver. Makes a good watch dragon; should not be allowed near children.

12 Narrowed-Eared Smut. Nervous and, therefore, short-lived.

13 The Lion-Headed Cowper. A large breed, easy to keep, but often afflicted with skiplets.

14 Tomkin's Neurovore. Handsome, but highly explosive due to nerves.

15 Porpoise-Headed Cowper. A breed for aficionados.

16 The Retiring Smut. Not often seen.

17 The Golden Rharn.

18 Birbright's Smut. Morbidly afraid of spoons.

19 Birbright's Lizard. Rare mountain breed, flightless.

20 Tabby Cowper. Best of the Cowpers, now quite popular.

21 Silver Regal. A classic breed, popular in Sto Lat.

22 Jessington's Blunt. Rare and very stupid.

23 Jessington's Deceiver. Small and better behaved than the Golden. Hoards pickle jars.

24 The Common Smut. The basic swamp dragon, familiar to all.

25 Pixy-faced Smut. Many congenital problems; for experts only.

26 The Flared Smut. Good with cabbage.

27 Horned Regal. Largely nocturnal, flightless, well-coloured, short in the wouters.

28 Smooth Deceiver. Good-natured, suitable for the smaller home.

29 Big-nosed Smut. Seldom breeds true. Attracted to mirrors.

30 Guttley's Leaper. Flightless, but can exceed 30mph running over open ground.

31 Spike-nosed Regal. One of the most beautiful of the classic dragons. Hates shoes.

32 Broken-faced Cowper. Seldom seen these days.

33 The Pique. Small, flightless, lives indoors. Eats only chicken and furniture.

34 Curly-maned Slottie. Amiable, tendency to slimp, seldom explosive.

35 Avery's 'Epolette', typical of the many miniature shoulder dragons.

36 Bridisian Courser. Not a very special dragon at all.

37, 38 Male and female Spouters, a breed that flies very badly but makes a suitable pet for the less discriminating household. Explodes in the presence of mint.

(from *The Show Judges' Guide to Dragons*, by Lady Sybil Ramkin, available from the Cavern Club Press, Ankh-Morpork, at AM$20)

t night rays of light shone through holes and gaps in the tarpaulin. Lord Vetinari wondered if Leonard was getting any sleep. It was quite possible that the man had designed some sort of contrivance to do it for him.

At the moment, there were other things to concern him.

The dragons were travelling in a ship of their own. It was far too dangerous to have them on board anything else. Ships were made of wood, and even when in a good mood dragons puffed little balls of fire. When they were over-excited, they exploded.

'They will be all right, won't they?' he said, keeping well back from the cages. 'If any of them are harmed I shall be in serious trouble with the Sunshine Sanctuary in Ankh-Morpork. This is not a prospect I relish, I assure you.'

'Mr da Quirm says there is no reason why they should not all get back safely, sir.'

'And would you, Mister Stibbons, trust yourself in a contrivance pushed along by dragons?'

Ponder swallowed. 'I'm not the stuff of heroes, sir.'

'And what causes this lack in you, may I ask?'

'I think it's because I've got an active imagination.'

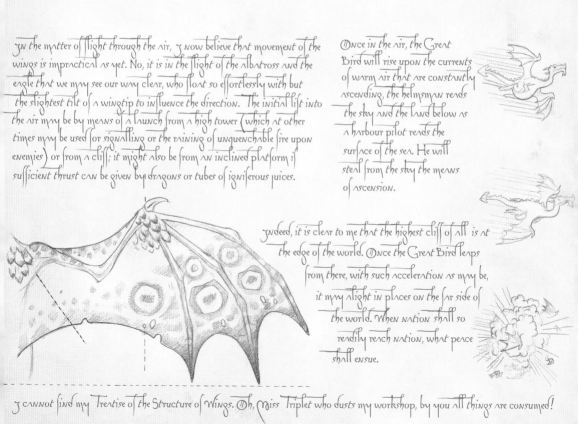

In the matter of flight through the air, I now believe that movement of the wings is impractical as yet. No, it is in the flight of the albatross and the eagle that we may see our way clear, who float so effortlessly with but the slightest tilt of a wingtip to influence the direction. The initial lift into the air may be by means of a launch from a high tower (which at other times may be used for signalling or the raining of unquenchable fire upon enemies) or from a cliff; it might also be from an inclined platform if sufficient thrust can be given by dragons or tubes of igniferous juices.

Once in the air, the Great Bird will rise upon the currents of warm air that are constantly ascending, the helmsman reads the sky and the land below as a harbour pilot reads the surface of the sea. He will steal from the sky the means of ascension.

Indeed, it is clear to me that the highest cliff of all is at the edge of the world. Once the Great Bird leaps from there, with such acceleration as may be, it may alight in places on the far side of the world. When nation shall so readily reach nation, what peace shall ensue.

I cannot find my Treatise of the Structure of Wings. Oh, Miss Triplet who dusts my workshop, by you all things are consumed!

This seemed a good explanation, Lord Vetinari mused as he walked away. The difference was that while other people imagined in terms of thoughts and pictures, Leonard imagined in terms of shape and space. His daydreams came with a cutting list and assembly instructions.

Lord Vetinari found himself hoping more and more for the success of his *other* plan. When all else fails, pray . . .

'All right now, lads, settle down. Settle down.' Hughnon Ridcully, Chief Priest of Blind Io, looked down at the multitude of priests and priestesses that filled the huge Temple of Small Gods. He shared many of the characteristics of his brother Mustrum. He also saw his job as being, essentially, one of organiser. There were plenty of people who were good at the actual *believing*, and he left them to it. It took a lot more than prayer to make sure the laundry got done and the building was kept in repair.

There were so many gods now . . . at least two thousand. Many were, of course, still very small. But you had to watch them. Gods were very much a fashion thing. Look at Om, now. One minute he was a bloodthirsty little deity in some mad hot country, and then suddenly he was one of the top gods. It had all been done by not answering prayers, but doing so in a sort of *dynamic* way that left open the possibility that one day he might and *then* there'd be fireworks. Hughnon, who had survived through decades of intense theological dispute by being a mean man at swinging a heavy thurible, was impressed by this novel technique.

And then, of course, you had your real newcomers like Aniger, Goddess of Squashed Animals. Who would have thought that better roads and faster carts would have led to that? But gods grew bigger when called upon at need, and enough minds had cried out, 'Oh god, what was that I hit?'

'Brethren!' he shouted, getting tired of waiting. 'And sistren!'

The hubbub died away. A few flakes of dry and crumbling paint drifted down from the ceiling.

'Thank you,' said Ridcully. 'Now, can you please listen? My colleagues and I' – and here he indicated the senior clergy behind him – 'have, I *assure* you, been working for some time on this idea, and there is no doubt that it is theologically sound. Can we *please* get on?'

He could still sense the annoyance among the priesthood. Born leaders didn't like being led.

'If we *don't* try this,' he tried, 'the godless wizards may succeed with *their* plans. And a fine lot of mugginses we will look.'

'This is all very well, but the form of things is important!' snapped a priest. 'We can't *all* pray at once! You *know* the gods don't like ecumenicalism! And what form of words will we use, pray?'

'I would have felt that a short non-controversial—' Hughnon Ridcully paused. In front of him were priests forbidden by holy edict from eating broccoli, priests who required unmarried girls to cover their ears lest they inflame the passions of other men, and priests who worshipped a small shortbread-and-raisin biscuit. *Nothing* was non-controversial.

'You see, it does appear that the world *is* going to end,' he said weakly.

'Well? Some of us have been expecting that for some considerable time! It will be a judgement on mankind for its wickedness!'

'And broccoli!'

'And the short haircuts girls are wearing today!'

'Only the biscuits will be saved!'

Ridcully waved his crozier frantically for silence.

'But this isn't the wrath of the gods,' he said. 'I did *tell* you! It's the work of a man!'

'Ah, but he may be the hand of a god!'

'It's Cohen the Barbarian,' said Ridcully.

'Even so, he might—'

The speaker in the crowd was nudged by the priest next to him.

'Hang on . . .'

There was a roar of excited conversation. There were few temples that hadn't been robbed or despoiled in a long life of adventuring, and the priests soon agreed that no god ever had anything in his hand that looked like Cohen the Barbarian. Hughnon turned his eyes up to the ceiling, with its beautiful but decrepit panorama of gods and heroes. Life must be a lot easier for gods, he decided.

'Very well,' said one of the objectors, haughtily. 'In that case, I think perhaps we could, in these special circumstances, get around a table just this once.'

'Ah, that *is* a good—' Ridcully began.

'But of course we will need to give some very *serious* consideration as to what shape the table is going to be.'

Ridcully looked blank for a moment. His expression did not change as he leaned down to one of his sub-deacons and said, 'Scallop, please have someone run along and tell my wife to pack my overnight bag, will you? I think this is going to take a little while . . .'

he central spire of Cori Celesti seemed to get no closer day by day.

'Are you sure Cohen's all right in the head?' said Evil Harry, as he helped Boy Willie manoeuvre Hamish's wheelchair over the ice.

''ere, are you tryin' to spread discontent among the troops, Harry?'

'Well, I did warn you, Will. I *am* a Dark Lord. I've got to keep in practice. And we're following a leader who keeps forgetting where he put his false teeth.'

'Whut?' said Mad Hamish.

'I'm just saying that blowing up the gods could cause trouble,' said Evil Harry. 'It's a bit . . . disrespectful.'

'You must've defiled a few temples in your time, Harry?'

'I *ran* 'em, Will, I *ran* 'em. I was a Mad Demon Lord for a while, you know. I had a Temple of Terror.'

'Yes, on your allotment,' said Boy Willie, grinning.

'That's right, that's right, rub it in,' said Harry sulkily. 'Just because I was never in the big league, just because—'

'Now, now, Harry, you know we don't think like that. We respected you. You knew the Code. You kept the faith. Well, Cohen just reckons the gods've got it comin' to them. Now, *me*, I'm worried because there's some tough ground ahead.'

Evil Harry peered along the snowy canyon.

'There's some kind of magic path leads up the mountain,' Willie went on. 'But there's a mass of caves before you get there.'

'The Impassable Caves of Dread,' said Evil Harry.

Willie looked impressed. 'Heard of them, have you? Accordin' to some old legend they're guarded by a legion of fearsome monsters and some devilishly devious devices and no one has *ever* passed through. Oh, yeah . . . perilous crevasses, too. Next, we'll have to swim through underwater caverns guarded by giant man-eating fish that no man has ever yet passed. And then there's some insane monks, and a door you can pass only by solving some ancient riddle . . . the usual sort of stuff.'

'Sounds like a big job,' Evil Harry ventured.

'Well, we know the answer to the riddle,' said Boy Willie. 'It's "teeth".'

'How did you find that out?'

'Didn't have to. It's *always* teeth in poxy old riddles.' Boy Willie grunted as they heaved the wheelchair through a particularly deep drift. 'But the biggest problem is going to be getting this damn thing through all that without Hamish waking up and making trouble.'

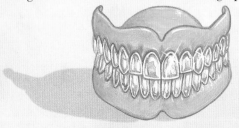

In the study of his dark house on the edge of Time, Death looked at the wooden box.

Perhaps I shall try one more time, he said.

He reached down and lifted up a small kitten, patted it on the head, lowered it gently into the box, and closed the lid.

The cat dies when the air runs out?

'I suppose it might, sir,' said Albert, his manservant. 'But I don't reckon that's the point. If I understand it right, you don't know if the cat's dead or alive until you look at it.'

Things will have come to a pretty pass, Albert, if *I* did not know whether a thing was dead or alive without having to go and look.

'Er . . . the way the theory goes, sir, it's the *act* of lookin' that determines if it's alive or not.'

Death looked hurt. Are you suggesting I will kill the cat just by looking at it?

'It's not quite like that, sir.'

I mean, it's not as if I make faces or anything.

'To be honest with you, sir, I don't think even the wizards understand the uncertainty business,' said Albert. 'We didn't truck with that class of stuff in my day. If you weren't certain, you were dead.'

Death nodded. It was getting hard to keep up with the times. Take parallel dimensions. *Parasite* dimensions, now, he understood *them*. He lived in one. They were simply universes that weren't quite complete in themselves and could only exist by clinging on to a host universe, like remora fish. But parallel dimensions meant that anything you did, you didn't do somewhere else.

This presented exquisite problems to a being who was, by nature, *definite*. It was like playing poker against an infinite number of opponents.

He opened the box and took out the kitten. It stared at him with the normal mad amazement of kittens everywhere.

I don't hold with cruelty to cats, said Death, putting it gently on the floor.

'I think the whole cat in the box idea is one of them metaphors,' said Albert.

Ah. A lie.

Death snapped his fingers.

Death's study did not occupy space in the normal sense of the word. The walls and ceiling were there for decoration rather than as any kind of dimensional limit. Now they faded away and a giant hourglass filled the air.

Its dimensions would be difficult to calculate, but they could be measured in miles.

Inside, lightnings crackled among the falling sands. Outside, a giant turtle was engraved upon the glass.

I think we shall have to clear the decks for this one, said Death.

vil Harry knelt in front of a hastily constructed altar. It consisted mostly of skulls, which were not hard to find in this cruel landscape. And now he prayed. In a long lifetime of being a Dark Lord, even in a small way, he'd picked up a few contacts on the other planes. They were . . . sort of gods, he supposed. They had names like Olk-Kalath the Soul Sucker, but frankly, the overlap between demons and gods was a bit uncertain at the best of times.

'Oh, Mighty One,' he began, always a safe beginning and the religious equivalent of 'To Whom It May Concern', 'I have to warn you that a bunch of heroes are climbing the mountain to destroy you with returned fire. May you strike them down with wrathful lightning and then look favourably upon thy servant, i.e. Evil Harry Dread. Mail may be left with Mrs Gibbons, 12 Dolmen View, Pant-y-Girdl, Llamedos. Also if possible I should like a location with real lava pits, every other evil lord manages to get a dread lava pit even when they are on one hundred feet of bloody alluvial soil, excuse my Klatchian, this is further discrimination against the small trader, no offence meant.'

He waited a moment, just in case there was any reply, sighed, and got rather shakily to his feet.

'I'm an evil, distrustful Dark Lord,' he said. 'What do they expect? I *told* 'em. I *warned* 'em. I mean, if it was up to me . . . but where'd I stand as a Dark Lord if I—'

His eye caught something pink, a little way off. He climbed a snow-covered rock for a better look.

Two minutes later the rest of the Horde had joined him and were looking at the scene reflectively, although the minstrel was being sick.

'Well, that's something you don't often see,' said Cohen.

'What, a man throttled with pink knitting wool?' said Caleb.

'No, I was looking at the other two . . . '

'Yes, it's amazing what you can do with a knitting needle,' said Cohen. He glanced back at the makeshift altar and grinned. 'Did you do this, Harry? You said you wanted to be alone.'

'Pink knitting wool?' said Evil Harry nervously. '*Me* and pink knitting wool?'

'Sorry for suggestin' it,' said Cohen. 'Well, we ain't got time for this. Let's go and sort out the Caves of Dread. Where's our bard? Right. Stop throwin' up and get yer notebook out. First man to be cut in half by a concealed blade is a rotten egg, okay? And, everyone . . . try not to wake up Hamish, all right?'

he sea was full of cool green light.

Captain Carrot sat near the prow. To the astonishment of Rincewind, who'd got out for a gloomy evening walk, he was sewing.

'It's a badge for the mission,' said Carrot. 'See? This is yours.' He held it up.

'But what is it *for*?'

'Morale.'

'Ah, that stuff,' said Rincewind. 'Well, you've got lots, Leonard doesn't need it and I've never had any.'

'I know you are being good-humoured about it, but I think it's vital that there is something that holds the crew together,' said Carrot, still calmly sewing.

'Yes, it's called skin. It's important to keep all of you on the inside of it.'

Rincewind stared at the badge. He'd never had one before. Well, that was technically a lie . . . he'd had one that said 'Hello, I Am **5** Today!', which was just about the worst possible present to get when you are six. That birthday had been the rottenest day of his life.

'It needs an uplifting motto,' said Carrot. 'Wizards know about this sort of thing, don't they?'

'How about *Morituri Nolumus Mori*, that's got the right ring,' said Rincewind gloomily.

Carrot's lips moved as he parsed the sentence. '*We who are about to die . . .* ' he said, 'but I don't recognise the rest.'

'It's very uplifting,' said Rincewind. 'It's straight from the heart.'

'Very well. Many thanks. I'll get to work on it right away,' said Carrot.

Rincewind sighed. 'You're finding this exciting, aren't you?' he said. 'You actually *are*.'

'It will certainly be a challenge to go where no one has gone before,' said Carrot.

'Wrong! We're going where no one has *come back from* before.' Rincewind hesitated. 'Well, except me. But I didn't go that far, and I . . . sort of dropped on to the Disc again.'

73

'Yes, they told me about it. What did you see?'

'My whole life, passing in front of my eyes.'

'Perhaps we shall see something more interesting.'

Rincewind glared at Carrot, bent once again over his sewing. Everything about the man was neat, in a workmanlike sort of way; he looked like someone who washed thoroughly. He also seemed to Rincewind to be a complete idiot with gristle between the ears. But complete idiots didn't make comments like that.

'I'm taking an iconograph and lots of paint for the imp. You know the wizards want us to make all kinds of observations?' Carrot went on. 'They say it's a once-in-a-lifetime opportunity.'

'You're not making any friends here, you know,' said Rincewind.

'Have you any idea what it is that the Silver Horde wants?'

'Drink, treasure, and women,' said Rincewind. 'But I think they may have eased back on the last one.'

'But didn't they have more or less all of that anyway?'

Rincewind nodded. That was the puzzler. The Horde had it all. They had everything that money could buy, and since there was a lot of money on the Counterweight Continent, that was *everything*.

It occurred to him that when you'd had everything, all that was left was nothing.

 he valley was full of cool green light, reflected off the towering ice of the central mountain. It shifted and flowed like water. Into it, grumbling and asking one another to speak up, walked the Silver Horde.

Behind them, walking almost bent double with horror and dread, white-faced, like a man who has gazed upon direful things, came the minstrel. His clothes were torn. One leg of his tights had been ripped off. He was soaking wet, although parts of his clothing were singed. The twanging remains of the lute in his trembling hand had been half bitten away. Here was a man who had truly seen life, mostly on the point of departure.

'Not *very* insane, as monks go,' said Caleb. 'More sad than mad. I've known monks that *frothed*.'

'And some of those monsters were long past their date with the knackerman, and that's the truth,' said Truckle. 'Honestly, I felt embarrassed about killing them. They was older than *us*.'

'The fish were good,' said Cohen. 'Real big buggers.'

'Just as well, really, since we've run out of walrus,' said Evil Harry.

'Wonderful display by your henchmen, Harry,' said Cohen. 'Stupidity wasn't the word for it. Never seen so many people hit themselves over the head with their own swords.'

'They were good lads,' said Harry. 'Morons to the end.'

Cohen grinned at Boy Willie, who was sucking a cut finger.

'Teeth,' he said. 'Huh . . . the answer is always "teeth", is it?'

'All right, all right, *sometimes* it's "tongue",' said Boy Willie. He turned to the minstrel.

'Did you get that bit where I cut up that big taranchula?' he said.

The minstrel raised his head slowly. A lute string broke.

'Mwwa,' he bleated.

The rest of the Horde gathered round quickly. There was no sense in letting just one of them get the best verses.

'*Remember to sing about that bit where that fish swallowed me and I cut my way out from inside, okay?*'

'Mwwa . . .'

'*And did you get that bit when I killed that big six-armed dancin' statue?*'

'Mwwa . . .'

'*What're you talkin' about? It was me what killed that statue!*'

'*Yeah? Well, I clove him clean in twain, mate. No one could have survived that!*'

'*Why didn't you just cut 'is 'ead orf?*'

'*Couldn't. Someone'd already done that.*'

'*'Ere, 'e's not writin' this down! Why isn't 'e writin' this down? Cohen, you tell 'im 'e's got to write this down!*'

'Let him be for a while,' said Cohen. 'I reckon the fish disagreed with him.'

'Don't see why,' said Truckle. 'I pulled him out before it'd hardly chewed him. And he must've dried out nicely in that corridor. You know, the one where the flames shot up out of the floor unexpectedly.'

'I reckon our bard wasn't expecting flames to shoot out of the floor unexpectedly,' said Cohen.

Truckle shrugged theatrically. '*Well*, if you're not going to expect unexpected flames, what's the point of going *anywhere*?'

Caleb
the Ripper

75

'And we'd have been in some strife with those gate demons from the netherworlds if Mad Hamish hadn't woken up,' Cohen went on.

Hamish stirred in his wheelchair, under a pile of large fish fillets inexpertly wrapped in saffron robes.

'Whut?'

'I SAID YOU WERE GROUCHY WHAT WITH MISSING YER NAP!' Cohen shouted.

'Ach, right!'

Boy Willie rubbed his thigh. 'I got to admit it, one of those monsters nearly got me,' he said. 'I'm going to have to give this up.'

Cohen turned around quickly. 'And die like old Old Vincent?' he said.

'Well, not—'

'Where would he have been if we weren't there to give him a *proper* funeral, eh? A great big bonfire, that's the funeral of a hero. And everyone else said it was a waste of a good boat! So stop talking like that and *follow me!*'

'Mw . . . mw . . . mw,' the minstrel sang, and finally the words came out. 'Mad! Mad! *Mad!* You're all stark staring *mad!*'

Caleb patted him gently on the shoulder as they turned to follow their leader.

'We prefer the word *berserk*, lad,' he said.

ome things needed testing . . .

'I have watched the swamp dragons at night,' Leonard said conversationally as Ponder Stibbons adjusted the static-firing mechanism. 'And it is clear to me that the *flame* is quite useful to them as a means of propulsion. In a sense, a swamp dragon is a living rocket. A strange creature to have come into being on a world like ours, I have always thought. I suspect they come from elsewhere.'

'They tend to explode a lot,' said Ponder, standing back. The dragon in the steel cage watched him carefully.

'Bad diet,' said Leonard firmly. 'Possibly not what they were used to. But I am sure the mixture I have devised is both nourishing *and* safe *and* will have . . . usable effect . . . '

'But we will go and get behind the sandbags *now*, sir,' said Ponder.

'Oh, do you really think—?'

'*Yes*, sir.'

With his back firmly against the sandbags, Ponder shut his eyes and pulled the string.

In front of the dragon's cage, a mirror swung down, just for a moment. And the first reaction of a male swamp dragon on seeing another male is to flame . . .

There was a roar. The two men peered over the barrier and saw a yellow-green lance of fire thundering out across the evening sea.

'Thirty-three seconds!' said Ponder, when it finally winked out. He leapt up.

The small dragon belched.

The flame was more or less gone, so it was the *dampest* explosion Ponder had ever experienced.

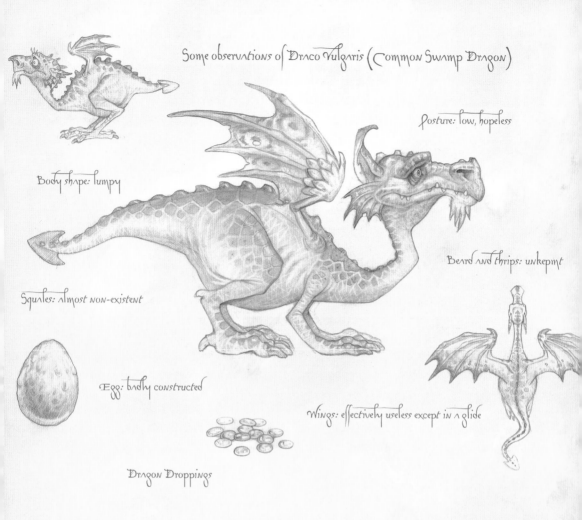

Some observations of Draco Vulgaris (Common Swamp Dragon)

Posture: low, hopeless

Body shape: lumpy

Beard and thrips: unkempt

Squales: almost non-existent

Egg: badly constructed

Wings: effectively useless except in a glide

Dragon Droppings

'Ah,' said Leonard, arising from behind the sandbags and peeling a piece of scaly skin off his head. 'Nearly there, I think. Just a pinch more charcoal and seaweed extract to prevent blowback.'

Ponder removed his hat. What he needed right now, he felt, was a bath. And then another bath.

'I'm not exactly a rocket wizard, am I?' he said, wiping bits of dragon off his face.

But an hour later another flame lanced over the waves, thin and white with a blue core . . . and this time, *this* time, the dragon merely smiled.

'**I**'d rather die than sign my name,' said Boy Willie.

'I'd rather face a dragon,' said Caleb. 'One of the proper old ones, too, not the little fireworky ones you get today.'

'Once they get you signin' your name, they've got you where they want you,' said Cohen.

'Too many letters,' said Truckle. 'All different shapes, too. I always put an X.'

The Horde had stopped for a breather and a smoke on an outcrop at the end of the green valley. Snow was thick on the ground, but the air was almost mild. Already there was the prickly sensation of a high magical field.

'Readin', now,' said Cohen, 'that's another matter. I don't mind a man who does a bit of *readin'*. Now, you come across a map, as it might be, and it's got a big cross on it, well, a readin' man can tell something from that.'

'What? That it's Truckle's map?' said Boy Willie.

'Exactly. Could very well be.'

'I can read *and* write,' said Evil Harry. 'Sorry. Part of the job. Etiquette, too. You've got to be *polite* to people when you march them out on the plank over the shark tank . . . it makes it more *evil*.'

'No one's blaming you, Harry,' said Cohen.

'Huh, not that I could *get* sharks,' said Harry. 'I should've known better when Johnny No Hands *told* me they were sharks that hadn't grown all their fins yet, but all they did was swim around squeaking happily and start beggin' for fish. When I throw people into a torture tank it's to be torn to bits, not to get in touch with their inner self and be one with the cosmos.'

'Shark'd be better than this fish,' said Caleb, making a face.

'Nah, shark tastes like piss,' said Cohen. He sniffed. 'Now *that* . . . '

'Now *that*,' said Truckle, 'is what I call *cookery*.'

They followed the smell through a maze of rocks to a cave. To the minstrel's amazement, each man drew his sword as they approached.

'You can't trust cookery,' said Cohen, apparently as an attempt at an explanation.

'But you've just been fighting monstrous mad devil fish!' said the minstrel.

'No, the priests were mad, the fish were . . . hard to tell with fish. Anyway, you know where you stand with a mad priest, but someone cooking as well as that right up here – well, that's a *mystery*.'

'Well?'

'Mysteries get you killed.'

'*You're* not dead, though.'

Cohen's sword swished through the air. The minstrel thought he heard it sizzle.

'I *solve* mysteries,' he said.

'Oh. With your sword . . . like Carelinus untied the Tsortean Knot?'

'Don't know anything about any knots, lad.'

In a clear space among the rocks, a stew was cooking over a fire and an elderly lady was

working at her embroidery. It was not a scene the minstrel would have expected out here, even though the lady was somewhat . . . *youngly* dressed for a grandmother, and the message on the sampler she was sewing, surrounded by little flowers, was EAT COLD STEEL PIGDOG.

'Well, well,' said Cohen, sheathing his sword. 'I *thought* I recognised the handiwork back there. How're you doing, Vena?'

'You're looking well, Cohen,' said the woman, as calmly as though she had been expecting them. 'You boys want some stew?'

'Yeah,' said Truckle, grinning. 'Let the bard try it first, though.'

'Shame on you, Truckle,' said the woman, putting aside her embroidery.

'Well, you *did* drug me and steal a load of jewels off me last time we met . . . '

'That was forty years ago, man! Anyway, *you* left me alone to fight that band of goblins.'

'I knew you'd beat the goblins, though.'

'I knew *you* didn't need the jewels. Morning, Evil Harry. Hello, boys. Pull up a rock. Who's the thin streak of misery?'

'This is the bard,' said Cohen. 'Bard, this is Vena the Raven-Haired.'

'What?' said the bard. 'No, she's not! Even I've heard of Vena the Raven-Haired, and she's a tall young woman with— Oh . . . '

Vena sighed. 'Yes, the old stories do hang around so, don't they?' she said, patting her grey hair. 'And it's Mrs McGarry now, boys.'

'Yes, I heard you'd settled down,' said Cohen, dipping the ladle into the stew and tasting it. 'Married an innkeeper, didn't you? Hung up your sword, had kids . . . '

'Grandchildren,' said Mrs McGarry, proudly. But then the proud smile faded. 'One of them's taken over the inn, but the other's a paper-maker.'

'Running an inn's a good trade,' said Cohen. 'But there's not much heroing in wholesale stationery. A paper cut's just not the same.' He smacked his lips. 'This is good stuff, girl.'

'It's funny,' said Vena. 'I never knew I had the talent, but people will come miles for my dumplings.'

'No change there, then,' said Truckle the Uncivil. 'Hur, hur, hur.'

'Truckle,' said Cohen, 'remember when you told me to tell you when you were bein' *too* uncivil?'

'Yeah?'

'That was one of those times.'

'Anyway,' said Mrs McGarry, smiling sweetly at the blushing Truckle, 'I was sitting around after Charlie died, and I thought, well, is this it? I've just got to wait for the Grim Reaper? And then . . . there was this scroll . . . '

'What scroll?' said Cohen and Evil Harry together. Then they stared at one another.

'Y'see,' said Cohen, reaching into his pack, 'I found this old scroll, showing a map of how to get to the mountain and all the little tricks for getting past—'

'Me too,' said Harry.

'You never told me!'

'I'm a *Dark Lord*, Cohen,' said Evil Harry patiently. 'I'm not *supposed* to be Captain Helpful.'

'Tell me where you found it, at least.'

'Oh, in some ancient sealed tomb we was despoilin'.'

'I found mine in an old storeroom back in the Empire,' said Cohen.

'*Mine* was left in my inn by a traveller all in black,' said Mrs McGarry.

In the silence, the minstrel said, 'Um? Excuse me?'

'What?' said all three together.

'Is it just me,' said the minstrel, 'or are we missing something here?'

'Like what?' demanded Cohen.

'Well, these scrolls all tell you how to get to the mountain, a peri-lous trek that no one has ever survived?'

'Yes? So?'

'So . . . um . . . who wrote the scrolls?'

A few of the Discworld gods, passing the time, as they do. *L to R:* Sessifet, Goddess of the afternoon, Offler the Crocodile God, Flatulus (God of the winds), Fate, Urika (Goddess of saunas, snow and theatrical performances for fewer than 120 people), Blind Io (chief of the Gods, and general Thundering), Libertina (Goddess of the sea, apple pie, certain types of ice cream and short lengths of string), The Lady (don't even ask), Bibulous (God of wine and things on sticks), Patina (*back*, Goddess of wisdom), Topaxi (*front*, God of certain mushrooms, and also of great ideas that you forgot to write down and will never remember again, and of people who tell other people that 'dog' is 'god' spelled backwards and think this is in some way revelatory), Bast (*back*, God of things left on the doorstep or half-digested under the bed), and Nuggan (a local god, but also in charge of paperclips, correct things in the right place in small desk stationery sets, and unnecessary paperwork).

Offler the Crocodile looked up from the playing board which was, in fact, the world.

'All right, who doth he belong to?' he lisped. 'We've got a *clever* one here.'

There was a general craning of necks among the assembled deities, and then one put up his hand.

'And you are . . . ?' said Offler.

'The Almighty Nuggan. I'm worshipped in parts of Borogravia. The young man was raised in my faith.'

'What do Nugganiteth believe in?'

'Er . . . me. Mostly me. And followers are forbidden to eat chocolate, ginger, mushrooms and garlic.'

Several of the gods winced.

'When you prohibit you don't meth about, do you?' said Offler.

'No sense in forbidding broccoli, is there? That sort of approach is very old-fashioned,' said Nuggan. He looked at the minstrel. 'He's never *been* particularly bright up till now. Shall I smite him? There's bound to be some garlic in that stew, Mrs McGarry looks the type.'

Offler hesitated. He was a very old god, who had arisen from steaming swamps in hot, dark lands. He had survived the rise and fall of more modern and certainly more beautiful gods by developing, for a god, a certain amount of wisdom.

Besides, Nuggan was one of the newer gods, all full of hellfire and self-importance and *ambition*. Offler was not bright, but he had some vague inkling that for long-term survival gods needed to offer their worshippers something more than a mere lack of thunderbolts. And he felt an ungodlike pang of sympathy for any human whose god banned chocolate *and* garlic. Anyway, Nuggan had an unpleasant moustache. No god had any business with a fussy little moustache like that.

'No,' he said, shaking the dice box. 'It'll add to the fun.'

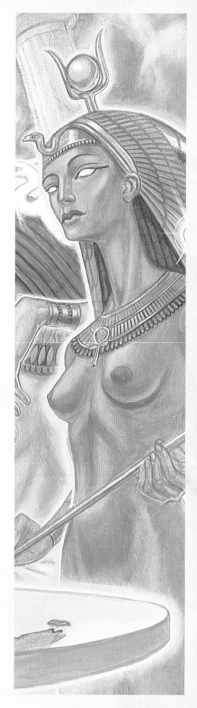Cohen pinched out the end of his ragged cigarette, stuffed it behind his ear and looked up at the green ice.

'It's not too late to turn back,' said Evil Harry. 'If anyone wanted to, I mean.'

'Yes it is,' said Cohen, without looking around. 'Besides, someone's not playing fair.'

'Funny, really,' said Vena. 'All my life I've gone adventuring with old maps found in old tombs and so on, and I never ever worried about where they came from. It's one of those things you never think about, like who leaves all the weapons and keys and medicine kits lying around in the unexplored dungeons.'

'Someone be setting a trap,' said Boy Willie.

'Probably. Won't be the first trap I've walked into,' said Cohen.

'We're going up against the gods, Cohen,' said Harry. 'A man does that, a man's got to be sure of his luck.'

'Mine's worked up to now,' said Cohen. He reached out and touched the rock face in front of him. 'It's warm.'

'But it's got ice on!' said Harry.

'Yeah. Strange, eh?' said Cohen. 'It's just like the scrolls said. And see the way the snow's sticking to it? It's the magic. Well . . . here goes . . . '

rchchancellor Ridcully decided that the crew needed to be trained. Ponder Stibbons pointed out that they were going into the completely unexpected, and Ridcully ruled therefore that they should be given some unexpected training.

Rincewind, on the other hand, said that they were heading for certain death, which everyone managed eventually with no training *whatsoever*.

Later he said that Leonard's device would do, though. After five minutes on it, certain death seemed like a release.

'He's thrown up *again*,' said the Dean.

'He's getting better at it, though,' said the Chair of Indefinite Studies.

'How can you say that? Last time it was a whole ten seconds before he let go!'

'Yes, but he's throwing up more, and it's going further,' said the Chair as they strolled away.

The Dean looked up. It was hard to see the flying device in the shadows of the tarpaulin-covered barge. Sheets were spread over the more interesting bits. There were strong smells of glue and varnish. The Librarian, who tended to get involved in things, was hanging peacefully from a spar and hammering wooden pegs into a plank.

Testing the Handiwork of the Gods

It being apparent that a voyage into the Great Void will result in much stress upon the human frame, I have devised this device of three rings that rotate continuously in three planes, giving the voyager the feeling of being rotated continuously in three planes. It is vital to know if the human body, or at least that of the wizard Rincewind, can withstand such treatment.

The Circulation of the Vomit

The wizard Rincewind reports a feeling of lightness occasioned by his stomach contents leaving his body and the wax running out of his ears. Prolonged tumbling on the device causes him to experience the feeling of wishing to kill everyone beginning, against all common sense, with himself. He also issues screams and threats. From this I deduce that being tumbled in three directions at once has a deleterious effect and I will arrange for this not to happen on the voyage. The musculature of the wizard Rincewind would make an interesting study if, indeed, he had any.

Leonard of
Quirm

'It'll be balloons, you mark my words,' said the Dean. 'I've got a mental picture. Balloons and sails and rigging and so on. Probably an anchor, too. Fanciful stuff.'

'Over in the Agatean Empire they have kites big enough to carry men,' said the Chair.

'Perhaps he's just building a bigger kite, then.'

In the distance Leonard of Quirm was sitting in a pool of light, sketching. Occasionally he'd hand a page to a waiting apprentice, who would hurry away.

'Did you see the design he came up with yesterday?' said the Dean. 'Had this idea that they might have to get outside the machine to repair it so – so he designed a sort of device to let you fly around with a dragon on your back! Said it was for emergencies!'

'What kind of emergency would be worse than having a dragon strapped to your back?' said the Chair of Indefinite Studies.

'Exactly! The man lives in an ivory tower!'

'Does he? I thought Vetinari had him locked up in some attic.'

'Well, I mean, years of that is going to give a man a very limited vision, in my humble opinion. Nothing much to do but tick the days off on the wall.'

'They say he paints good pictures,' said the Chair.

'Well, *pictures*,' said the Dean dismissively.

'But they say that his are so good the eyes follow you round the room.'

'Really? What does the rest of the face do?'

'*That* stays where it is, I suppose,' said the Chair of Indefinite Studies.

'To me, this does not sound good,' said the Dean as they wandered out into the daylight.

At his desk, while considering the problem of steering a craft in thin air, Leonard carefully drew a rose.

vil Harry shut his eyes.

'This does not feel good,' he said.

'It's easy when you get used to it,' said Cohen. 'It's just a matter of how you look at things.'

Evil Harry opened his eyes again.

He was standing on a broad, greenish plain, which curved down gently to right and left. It was like being on a high, grassy ridge. It stretched off into a cloudy distance.

'It's just a stroll,' said Boy Willie, beside him.

'Look, my feet aren't the problem here,' said Evil Harry. 'My feet aren't quarrelling. It's my brain.'

'It helps if you think of the ground as being *behind* you,' said Boy Willie.

'No,' said Evil Harry. 'It doesn't.'

The strange feature of the mountain was this: once a foot was set on it, direction became a matter of personal choice. To put it another way, gravity was optional. It stayed under your feet, no matter which way your feet were pointing.

Evil Harry wondered why it was affecting only him. The Horde seemed entirely unmoved. Even Mad Hamish's horrible wheelchair was bowling along happily in a direction which, up until now, Harry had thought of as vertical. It was, he thought, probably because Evil Lords were generally brighter than heroes. You needed some functioning brain cells to do the payroll, even for half a dozen henchmen. And Evil Harry's braincells were telling him to look straight ahead and try to believe that he *was* strolling along a broad, happy ridge *and on no account* to turn around, to even *think* about turning round, because *behind* him was gnh gnh gnh . . .

'Steady on!' said Boy Willie, steadying his arm. 'Listen to your feet. They know what they're about.'

To Harry's horror, Cohen chose this moment to turn around.

'Will you look at that view!' he said. 'I can see *everybody's* house from up here!'

'Oh, no, please, no,' mumbled Evil Harry, flinging himself forward and holding on to the mountain.

'It's great, isn't it?' said Truckle. 'Seein' all them seas sort of hanging right over you like— What's up with Harry?'

'Just a bit poorly,' said Vena.

To Cohen's surprise, the minstrel seemed quite at home with the view.

'I came from up in the mountains,' he explained. 'You get a head for heights up there.'

'I bin to everywhere I can see,' said Cohen, looking around. 'Been there, done that . . . been there again, done it twice . . . nowhere left where I ain't been . . .'

The minstrel looked him up and down, and a kind of understanding dawned. I know why you are doing this

now, he thought. Thank goodness for a classical education. Now, what was the quote?

'"And Carelinus wept, for there were no more worlds to conquer",' he said.

'Who's that bloke? You mentioned him before,' said Cohen.

'You haven't heard of the Emperor Carelinus?'

'Nope.'

'But . . . he was the greatest conquerer that ever lived! His empire spanned the entire Disc! Except for the Counterweight Continent and Fourecks, of course.'

'I don't blame him. You can't get a good beer in one of 'em for love nor money, and the other's a bugger to get to.'

'Well, when he got as far as the coast of Muntab, it was said that he stood on the shore and wept. Some philosopher told him there were more worlds out there somewhere, and that he'd never be able to conquer them. Er . . . that reminded me a bit of you.'

Cohen strolled along in silence for a moment.

'Yeah,' he said at last. 'Yeah, I can see how that could be. Only not as cissy, obviously.'

'It is now,' said Ponder Stibbons, 'T minus twelve hours.'

His audience, sitting on the deck, watched him with alert and polite incomprehension.

'That means the flying machine will go over the Edge just before dawn tomorrow,' Ponder explained.

Everyone turned to Leonard, who was watching a seagull.

'Mr da Quirm?' said Lord Vetinari.

'What? Oh. Yes.' Leonard blinked. 'Yes. The device will be ready, although the privy is giving me problems.'

The Lecturer in Recent Runes fumbled in the capacious pockets of his robe. 'Oh dear, I believe I have a bottle of something . . . the sea always affects me that way, too.'

'I was rather thinking of problems associated with the thin air and low gravity,' said Leonard. 'That's what the survivor of the *Maria Pesto* reported. But this afternoon I feel I can come up with a privy that, happily, utilises the thinner air of altitude to achieve the effect normally associated with gravity. Gentle suction is involved.'

Ponder nodded. He had a quick mind when it came to mechanical detail, and he'd already formed a mental picture. Now a mental eraser would be useful.

'Er . . . good,' he said. 'Well, most of the ships will fall behind the barge during the night. Even with magically assisted wind we dare not venture closer than thirty miles to the Rim. After that, we could be caught in the current and swept over the Edge.'

Rincewind, who had been leaning moodily over the rail and watching the water, turned at this.

'How far are we from the island of Krull?' he said.

'That place? Hundreds of miles,' said Ponder. 'We want to keep *well* away from those pirates.'

'So . . . we'll run straight into the Circumfence, then?'

There was technically silence, although it was loud with unspoken thoughts. Each man was busy trying to think of a reason why it would have been far too much to expect *him* to have thought of this, while at the same time being a reason why someone else *should* have. The Circumfence was the biggest construction ever built; it extended almost a third of the way around the world. On the large island of Krull, an entire civilisation lived on what they recovered from it. They ate a lot of sushi, and their dislike for the rest of the world was put down to permanent dyspepsia.

In his chair, Lord Vetinari grinned in a thin, acid way.

'Yes indeed,' he said. 'It extends for several thousands of miles, I understand. However, I gather the Krullians no longer keep captive seamen as slaves. They simply charge ruinous salvage rates.'

'A few fireballs would blow the thing apart,' said Ridcully.

'That does rather require you to be very close to it, though,' said Lord Vetinari. 'That is to say, so close to the Rimfall that you would be destroying the very thing that is preventing you from being swept over the Edge. A knotty problem, gentlemen.'

'Magic carpet,' said Ridcully. 'Just the job. We've got one in—'

'Not that close to the Edge, sir,' said Ponder, dismally. 'The thaumic field is very thin and there are some ferocious air currents.'

There was the crisp rattle of a big drawing pad being turned to the next page.

'Oh, yes,' said Leonard, more or less to himself.

'Pardon me?' said the Patrician.

'I did once design a simple means whereby entire fleets could be destroyed quite easily, my lord. Only as a technical exercise, of course.'

'But with numbered parts and a list of instructions?' said the Patrician.

'Why, *yes*, my lord. Of course. Otherwise it would not be a proper exercise. And I feel sure that with the help of these magical gentlemen we should be able to adapt it for this purpose.'

He gave them a bright smile. They looked at his drawing. Men were leaping from ships in flames, into a boiling sea.

'You do this sort of thing as a hobby, do you?' said the Dean.

'Oh, yes. There are no practical applications.'

'But couldn't someone *build* something like that?' said the Lecturer in Recent Runes. 'You practically include glue and transfers!'

'Well, I daresay there are people like that,' said Leonard diffidently. 'But I am sure the government would put a stop to things before they went too far.'

And the smile on Lord Vetinari's face was one that probably even Leonard of Quirm, with all his genius, would never be able to capture on canvas.

Very carefully, knowing that if they dropped one they probably wouldn't even *know* they'd dropped one, a team of students and apprentices lifted the cages of dragons into the racks under the rear of the flying machine.

Occasionally one of the dragons hiccuped. Everyone present, bar one, would freeze. The exception was Rincewind, who would be crouched down behind a pile of timber many yards away.

'They've all been well fed on Leonard's special feed and should be quite docile for four or five hours,' said Ponder, pulling him out for the third time. 'The first two stages were given their meals with a carefully timed interval, and the first lot should be in a mood to flame just as you go over the Rimfall.'

'What if we're delayed?'

Ponder gave this some deep thought.

'Whatever you do, don't be delayed,' he said.

'Thank you.'

'The ones that you'll be taking with you in flight may need feeding, too. We've loaded a mixture of naphtha, rock oil and anthracite dust.'

'For me to feed to the dragons.'

'Yes.'

'In this wooden ship, which will be very, very high?'

'Well, in a technical sense, yes.'

'Could we focus on that technicality?'

'Strictly speaking, there won't be any down. As such. Er . . . you could say that you will be travelling so fast that you won't be in any one place long enough to fall down.' Ponder sought a glimmer of understanding in Rincewind's face. 'Or, to put in another way, you'll be falling permanently without ever hitting the ground.'

Up above them, rack on rack of dragons sizzled contentedly. Wisps of steam drifted through the shadows.

'Oh,' said Rincewind.

'You understand?' said Ponder.

'No. I was just hoping that if I didn't say anything you'd stop trying to explain things to me.'

'How are we doing, Mr Stibbons?' said the Archchancellor, strolling up at the head of his wizards. 'How's our enormous kite?'

'Everything's going to plan, sir. We're at T minus five hours, sir.'

'Really? Good. We're at supper in ten minutes.'

Rincewind had a small cabin, with cold water and running rats. Most of it that wasn't occupied by his bunk was occupied by his luggage. The Luggage.

It was a box that walked around on hundreds of little legs. It was magical, as far as he knew. He'd had it for years. It understood every word he said. It obeyed about one in every hundred, unfortunately.

'There won't be any *room*,' he said. 'And you know every time you've gone up in the air you've got lost.'

The Luggage watched him in its eyeless way.

'So you stay with nice Mr Stibbons, all right? You've never been at ease around gods, either. I shall be back very soon.'

Still the eyeless stare went on.

'Just don't *look* at me that way, will you?' said Rincewind.

Lord Vetinari cast his eye over the three . . . what was the word?

'Men,' he said, settling for one that was undoubtedly correct, 'it falls to me to congratulate you on . . . on . . . '

He hesitated. Lord Vetinari was not a man who delighted in the technical. There were two cultures, as far as he was concerned. One was the real one, the other was occupied by people who liked machinery and ate pizza at unreasonable hours.

' . . . on being the first people to leave the Disc with the resolute intention of returning to it,' he went on. 'Your . . . mission is to land on or near Cori Celesti, locate Cohen the Barbarian and his men, and by whatever means feasible stop this ridiculous scheme of theirs. There must be some misunderstanding. Even barbarian heroes generally draw the line at blowing up the world.' He sighed. 'They're usually not civilised enough for that,' he added. 'Anyway . . . we implore him to listen to reason, et cetera. Barbarians are generally sentimentalists. Tell him about all the dear little puppies that will be killed, or something. Beyond that, I can't advise you further. I suspect classical force is out of the question. If Cohen was easy to kill, people would have done it a long time ago.'

Captain Carrot saluted. 'Force is always the last resort, sir,' he said.

'I believe that for Cohen it's the first choice,' said Lord Vetinari.

'He's not too bad if you don't come up behind him suddenly,' said Rincewind.

'Ah, there is the voice of our mission specialist,' said the Patrician. 'I just hope— What is that on your badge, Captain Carrot?'

'Mission motto, sir,' said Carrot cheerfully. '*Morituri Nolumus Mori*. Rincewind suggested it.'

'I imagine he did,' said Lord Vetinari, observing the wizard coldly. 'And would you care to give us a colloquial translation, Mr Rincewind?'

'Er . . . ' Rincewind hesitated, but there really was no escape. 'Er . . . roughly speaking, it means, "We who are about to die don't want to", sir.'

'Very clearly expressed. I commend your determination . . . Yes?'

Ponder had whispered something in his ear.

'Ah, I'm informed that we have to leave you shortly,' said Lord Vetinari. 'Mr Stibbons tells me that there is a means of keeping in touch with you, at least until you're close to the mountain.'

'Yes, sir,' said Carrot. 'The fractured omniscope. An amazing device. Each part sees what the other parts see. Astonishing.'

'Well, I trust your new careers will be uplifting if not, ahaha, meteoric. To your places, gentlemen.'

'Er . . . I just want to take an iconograph, sir,' said Ponder, hurrying forward and clutching a large box. 'To record the moment? If you would all stand in front of the flag and smile, please . . . that means the corners of your mouth go *up*, Rincewind . . . thank you.' Ponder, like all bad photographers, took the shot just a fraction of a second *after* the smiles had frozen. 'And do you have any last words?'

'You mean, last words before we go and come back?' said Carrot, his brow wrinkling.

'Oh, yes. Of course. That's what I meant! Because of course you will be coming back, won't you?' said Ponder, far too quickly in Rincewind's opinion. 'I have absolute confidence in Mr da Quirm's work, and I'm sure he has too.'

'Oh, dear. No, I never bother to have any confidence,' said Leonard.

'You don't?'

'No, things just work. You don't have to wish,' said Leonard. 'And, of course, if we *do* fail, then things won't be that bad, will they? If we fail to come back, there won't be anywhere left to fail to come back *to* in any case, will there? So it will all cancel out.' He gave his happy little smile. 'Logic is a great comfort in times like this, I always find.'

'Personally,' said Captain Carrot, 'I am happy, thrilled and delighted to be going.' He tapped a box by his side. 'And I am, as instructed, also bringing along an iconograph and intend to take many useful and deeply moving images of our world from the perspective of space which will perhaps cause us to see humanity in an entirely new light.'

'Is this the time to resign from the crew?' said Rincewind, staring at his fellow voyagers.

'No,' said Lord Vetinari.

'Possibly on grounds of insanity?'

'Your own, I assume?'

'Take your pick!'

Vetinari beckoned Rincewind forward.

'But it could be said that someone would have to *be* insane to take part in this venture,' he murmured. 'In which case, of course, you are fully qualified.'

'Then . . . supposing I'm *not* insane?'

'Oh, as ruler of Ankh-Morpork I have a duty to send only the keenest, coolest minds on a vital errand of this kind.'

He held Rincewind's gaze for a moment.

'I think there's a catch there,' said the wizard, knowing that he'd lost.

'Yes. The best kind there is,' said the Patrician.

he lights of the anchored ships disappeared into the murk as the barge drifted on, faster now as the current began to pull.

'No turning back now,' said Leonard.

There was a roll of thunder, and fingers of lightning walked along the Edge of the world.

'Just a squall, I expect,' he added, as fat drops of rain thudded on the tarpaulins. 'Shall we get aboard? The draglines will keep us pointed directly at the Rim, and we might as well make ourselves comfortable while we wait.'

'We ought to release the fire boats first, sir,' said Carrot.

'Silly me, yes,' said Leonard. 'I'd forget my own head if it wasn't held on with bones and skin and things!'

A The helmsman's chair

B Left wing chair

C Right wing chair (for mission specialist)

D Yoke (for altitude and wing-warping)

E Pedals (for rudder)

F Device for Looking Behind You

G Fragment of omniscope

H Sphere of quicksilver (to show ground level)

I Wing winding handle

J Dragon Blinkers handle

K Mirror Array handle

L Salmon of Thunder mirror release

M Salmon of Thunder Separation

N Dragon Pod Separation

O Device for Slowing Instantly

P Troba (wing jettison, endeavour not to use)

Q Windscreen wiper

R Seat adjuster

S Prince Haran's Tiller

T Wing capstan release

U Cup holders

Editor's note: Just like Leonardo da Vinci, Leonard of Quirm famously wrote backwards, a talent not unusual in left-handed people. Sadly, but for the purpose of clarity and the continued sanity of our readers, we have been forced to print the handwriting the wrong way round.

That a man may fly to the edges of the world and beyond. I find that if this instrument be well made, and hurled with sufficient force over the endless rim, it will put a ring around the world. And the first flight of the Great Bird to the summit of Monte Celesti will fill the universe with wonder.

...olt of Bird's Eye
...ple at 12.0 a foot.

The cabin for the crew, sealed against the egress of air (see drawings A18-25)

The cabin may detach and float should the Great Bird land in the sea. Extra dragons to allow it to fly home alone? Mem: no.

of gravity
...on flame
...culated
...te!!
Superque!

When a bird finds itself within the wind, it can sustain itself above it without beating its wings. By means of capstans and strings under tension, my wings will take any shape desired, both for gliding and stooping, de plano.

The fixed wings of wood and canvas, contrived to change their shape in accordance with the wishes of the steersman (see drawings A10-14)

There are to be cradles for dragons, for the propulsion caused by the flames thereof.

I recall my great pleasure upon seeing a fish eagle stoop upon a salmon in a lake and then, upon rising again, turn the salmon in its talons so that the head of the salmon was facing forwards. For it demonstrates that the air and water are, in their currents and pressures, both fluids of a kind, which cause the denizens to develop certain similarities of form, the better to navigate these fluids.

The Bird in free flight
Aspects of the Bird stooping, wings in folded position the better to countenance the resistive forces of the air. Below the wings may be seen the small dragon 'pods' to allow steering and power in the thin air during the ring path around the World (see drawings B1-B18)

The additional tail for the first part of the voyage shall detach when no longer required (Mem: too small, too small. There must be more power!)

Seal of gutta-percha? Wood finish of Spirits of Kelp, then No.2 varnish, then No. 00 varnish.

The Great Bird is the eagle; between its talons it grips the Salmon of Thunder. The tail section powers the assemblage beyond the fractious air currents of the Rim, and then detaches (see drawing A2)

$67 \times 2 + 89 = 223$ galls.
2,000 sheathed bronze nails.

The body of the Salmon. It is segmented, to allow array after array of male dragons to be induced to flame by the mirror mechanisms. Each segment is then discarded. (see drawing A7)

If crew and cabin cargo were reduced, the Bird could carry barrels of explosive powders, Ephebian fire and other instruments of War to rain terror upon enemy cities without fear of retaliation (see drawings B20 to G34; chemical recipes, Notebook 14). Happily, no government would ever allow such madness, and the flight of many Birds could only bring international peace and brotherhood.

A couple of ship's boats had been sacrificed for the attempt on the Circumfence. They wallowed slightly, laden as they were with spare tins of varnish, paint and the remains of the dragons' supper. Carrot picked up a couple of lanterns and, after a couple of tries in the gusting wind, managed to light them and place them carefully according to Leonard's instructions.

Then the boats were cast adrift. Freed of the drag of the barge, they pulled away in the quickening current.

The rain was hammering down now.

'And *now* let us get aboard,' said Leonard, ducking back out of the rain. 'A cup of tea will do us good.'

'I thought we decided we couldn't have any naked flames on board, sir,' said Carrot.

'I have brought along a special jug of my own devising which keeps things warm,' said Leonard. 'Or cold, if you prefer. I call it the Hot or Cold Flask. I am at a loss as to how it knows which it *is* that you prefer, but nevertheless it seems to work.'

He led the way up the ladder.

Only one small lamp lit the little cabin. It illuminated three seats, embedded among a network of levers, armatures and springs.

The crew had been up here before. They knew the layout. There was one little bed further aft, on the basis that there would only be *time* for any one person to be asleep. String bags had been stapled to every bit of unused wall to hold water bottles and food. Unfortunately, some of Lord Vetinari's committees, devised in order to prevent their members from interfering with anything important, had turned their attention to provisioning the craft. It appeared packed for every eventuality, including alligator-wrestling on a glacier.

Leonard sighed.

'I really didn't like to say no to anyone,' he said. 'I *did* suggest that, er, nourishing but concentrated and, er, low-residue food would be preferred—'

As one man, they turned in their seats to look at the Experimental Privy Mk 2. Mk 1 had worked – Leonard's devices tended to – but since a key to its operation was that it tumbled very fast on a central axis while in use it had been abandoned after a report by its test pilot (Rincewind) that, whatever you had in mind when you went in, the only thing you wanted to do once inside was get out.

Mk 2 was as yet untried. It creaked ominously under their gaze, an open invitation to constipation and kidney stones.

'It will undoubtedly function,' said Leonard, and just this once Rincewind noted the harmonic of uncertainty. 'It is all just a matter of opening the correct valves in sequence.'

'What happens if we don't open the right valves in sequence, sir?' said Carrot, buckling himself in.

'You must appreciate that I have had to design so many things for this craft—' Leonard began.

'We'd still like to know,' said Rincewind.

'Er . . . in truth, what happens if you don't open the right valves in sequence is that you will wish you *had* opened the right valves in sequence,' said Leonard. He fumbled below his seat and produced a large metal flask of curious design. 'Tea, anyone?' he said.

'Just a small cup,' said Carrot firmly.

'Make mine a spoonful,' said Rincewind. 'And what's this thing hanging in the ceiling in front of me?'

'It's my new device for looking behind you,' said Leonard. 'It's very simple to use. I call it the Device For Looking Behind You.'

'Looking behind you is a bad move,' said Rincewind firmly. 'I've always said so. It slows you down.'

'Ah, but this way we won't slow down at all.'

'Really?' said Rincewind, brightening up.

A squall of rain banged on the tarpaulins. Carrot tried to see ahead. A gap had been cut in the covers so that the—

'By the way . . . what *are* we?' he said. 'I mean, what do we call ourselves?'

'Possibly foolish,' said Rincewind.

'I meant *officially*.' Carrot looked around the crammed cabin. 'And what do we call this craft?'

'The wizards call it the big kite,' said Rincewind. 'But it's nothing like a kite, a kite is something on a string which—'

'It has to *have* a name,' said Carrot. 'It's very bad luck to attempt a voyage in a vessel with no name.'

Rincewind looked at the levers in front of his seat. They had to do mainly with dragons. 'We're in a big wooden box and behind us are about a hundred dragons who are getting ready to burp,' he said. 'I think we *need* a name. Er . . . do you actually know *how* to fly this thing, Leonard?'

'Not as such, but I intend to learn very soon.'

'A really *good* name,' said Rincewind fervently. Ahead of them the stormy horizon was lit by an explosion. The boats had hit the Circumfence, and burst into fierce, corrosive flame. 'Right *now*,' he added.

'The kite, the *real* kite, is a very beautiful bird,' said Leonard. 'It's what I had in mind when I—'

'The *Kite* it is, then,' said Carrot firmly. He glanced at a list pinned in front of him and ticked off one item. 'Shall I drop the tarpaulin anchor, sir?'

'Yes. Er. Yes. Do that,' said Leonard. Carrot pulled a lever. Below and behind them there was the sound of a splash, and then of cable running out very fast.

'There's a reef! There's rocks!' Rincewind stood up, pointing.

The firelight ahead glowed on something squat and immovable, surrounded by surf.

'No turning back,' said Leonard as the sinking anchor dragged the *Kite*'s coverings off like an enormous canvas egg. He reached out and pulled handles and knobs like an organist in full fugue.

'Number One Blinkers . . . down. Tethers . . . off. Gentlemen, each pull those big handles beside you when I say . . . '

The rocks loomed. The white water at the lip of the endless Fall was red with fire and glowing with lightning. Jagged rocks were a few yards away, hungry as a crocodile's teeth.

'Now! Now! Now! Mirrors . . . down! Good! We have flame! Now what was it . . . oh, yes . . . *Everyone hold on to something!*'

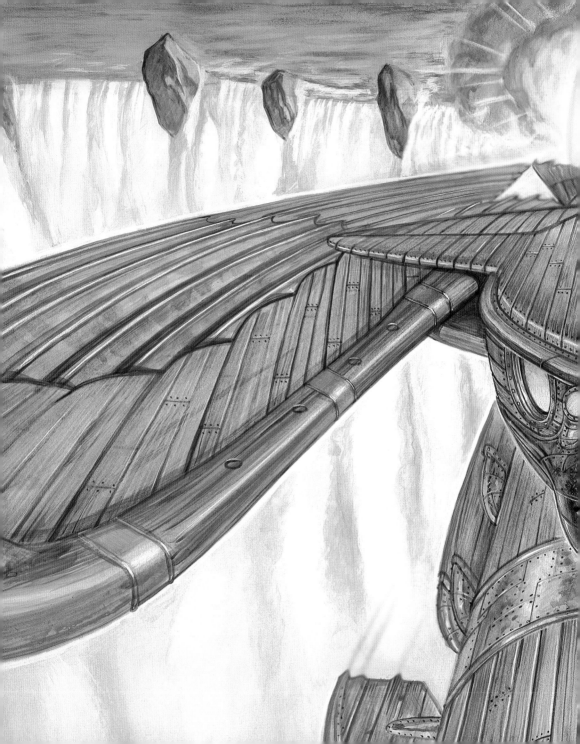

Wings unfolding, dragons flaring, the *Kite* rose from the splintering barge and into the storm and over the Rim of the world . . .

The only sound was a faint whisper of air as Rincewind and Carrot clambered off the shivering floor. Their pilot was staring out of the window.

'Look at the birds! Oh, do look at the birds!'

In the calm sunlit air beyond the storm they swooped and turned in their thousands around the gliding ship, as small birds will mob an eagle. And it did *look* like an eagle, one that had just snatched a giant salmon from the Fall . . .

Leonard stood entranced, tears running down his cheeks.

Carrot tapped him very gently on the shoulder. 'Sir?'

'It's so beautiful . . . so beautiful . . . '

'Sir, we need you to fly this thing, sir! Remember? Stage Two?'

'Hmm?' Then the artist shuddered, and part of him returned to his body. 'Oh, yes, very well, very well . . . ' He sat down heavily in his seat. 'Yes . . . to be sure . . . yes. We shall, er, we shall test the controls. Yes.'

He laid a trembling hand on the levers in front of him, and placed his feet on the pedals. The *Kite* lurched sideways on the air.

'Oops . . . ah, now I think I have it . . . sorry . . . yes . . . oh, sorry, dear me . . . ah, now I think . . . '

Rincewind, flung against the window by another judder, looked down the face of the Rimfall.

Here and there, all the way down, mountain-sized islands projected from the wall of white water, glowing in the evening light. Little white clouds scudded between them. And everywhere there were birds, wheeling, nesting, gliding—

'There's *forests* on those rocks! They're like little countries . . . there's *people*! I can see *houses*!'

He was thrown back again as the *Kite* banked into some cloud.

'There's *people* living over the Edge!' he said.

'Old shipwrecks, I suppose,' said Carrot.

'I, er, I think I have the hang of it now,' said Leonard, staring fixedly ahead. 'Rincewind, please be so good as to pull that lever there, will you?'

Rincewind did so. There was a clunk behind them, and the ship shook slightly as the first-stage cage was dropped.

As it tumbled slowly apart in the air, small dragons spread their wings and flapped hopefully back towards the Disc.

'I thought there would be more than that,' said Rincewind.

'Oh, those are just the ones we used to help us get clear of the Rim,' said Leonard, as the *Kite* turned lazily in the air. 'Most of the others we'll use to go down.'

'Down?' said Rincewind.

'Oh, yes. We need to go down, as quickly as we can. No time to waste.'

'Down? This is not the time to talk about *down*! You kept on talking about *around*. Around is fine! Not *down*!'

'Ah, but you see, in order to go *around* we need to go *down*. Fast.' Leonard looked reproachful. 'I did put it in my notes—'

'*Down* is not a direction with which I am happy!'

'Hello? Hello?' came a voice, out of the air.

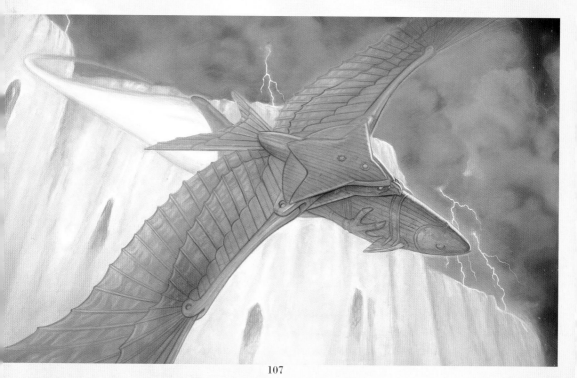

'Captain Carrot,' said Leonard, as Rincewind sulked in his seat, 'oblige me by opening the cabinet there, will you?'

This revealed a fragment of smashed omniscope and the face of Ponder Stibbons.

'It works!' His shout sounded muffled and somehow small, like the squeaking of an ant. 'You're alive?'

'We have separated the first dragons and everything is going well, sir,' said Carrot.

'No, it's not!' Rincewind shouted. 'They want to go dow—!'

Without turning his head, Carrot reached around behind Leonard and pulled Rincewind's hat down over his face.

'The second-stage dragons will be about ready to burn now,' said Leonard. 'We had better get on, Mr Stibbons.'

'Please take careful observations of all—' Ponder began, but Leonard had politely closed the case.

'Now then,' he said, 'if you gentlemen will undo the clips beside you and turn the large red handles you should be able to start the process of folding the wings back in. I believe that as we increase speed the impellers will make the process easier.' He looked at Rincewind's blank face as the angry wizard freed himself from his hat. 'We will use the rushing air as we fall to help us reduce the size of the wings, which we will not require for a while.'

'I *understand* that,' said Rincewind distantly. 'I just *hate* it.'

'The only way home is down, Rincewind,' said Carrot, adjusting his seat belt. 'And put your helmet on!'

'So if everyone would once again hold tight?' said Leonard, and pushed gently on a lever. 'Don't look so worried, Rincewind. Think of it as a sort of . . . well, a magic carpet ride . . .'

The *Kite* shuddered.

And dived . . .

And suddenly the Rimfall was *under* them, stretching to an infinite misty horizon, its rocky outcrops now islands in a white wall.

The ship shook again, and the handle Rincewind had been leaning on started to move under its own power.

There was no solid surface any more. Every piece of the ship was vibrating.

He stared out of the porthole next to him. The wings, the precious wings, the things that kept you *up*, were folding gracefully in on themselves . . .

'Rrincewwind,' said Leonard, a blur in his seat, 'pplease ppull the bblack lleverr!'

The wizard did so, on the basis that it couldn't make things worse.

But it did. He heard a series of thumps behind him. Five-score of dragons, having recently digested a hydrocarbon-rich meal, saw their own reflections in front of them as a rack of mirrors was, for a moment, lowered in front of their cages.

They flared.

Something crashed and smashed, back in the fuselage. A giant foot pressed the crew back into their seats. The Rimfall blurred. Through red-rimmed eyes they stared at the speeding white sea and the distant stars and even Carrot joined in the hymn of terror, which goes:

'Aaaaaaaaaahhhhhhhhhhhgggggggg . . . '

Leonard was trying to shout something. With terrible effort Rincewind turned his huge and heavy head and just made out the groan: 'Ttthe wwwhite lllever!'

It took him years to reach it. For some reason his arms had been made out of lead. Bloodless fingers with muscles weak as string managed to get a grip and tow the lever back.

Another foreboding thump rattled the ship. The pressure ceased. Three heads thumped forward.

And then there was silence. And lightness. And peace.

Dreamily, Rincewind pulled down the periscope and saw the huge fish section curving gently away from them. It came apart as it flew, and more dragons spread their wings and whirled away behind the *Kite*. Magnificent. A device for seeing behind you without slowing down? Just the thing no coward should be without.

'I've got to get one of these,' he murmured.

'That seemed to go quite well, I thought,' said Leonard. 'I'm sure the little creatures will get back, too. Flitting from rock to rock . . . yes, I'm sure they will . . . '

'Er . . . there's a strong draught by my seat—' Carrot began.

'Ah, yes . . . it would be a good idea to keep the helmets handy,' Leonard said. 'I've done my best, varnishing and laminating and so forth . . . but the *Kite* is not, alas, completely airtight. Well, here we are, well on our way,' he added brightly. 'Breakfast, anyone?'

'My stomach feels very—' Rincewind began, but stopped.

A spoon drifted past, tumbling gently.

'What has switched off the down-ness?' he demanded.

Leonard opened his mouth to say: No, this was expected, because everything is falling at the same speed, but he didn't, because he could see this was not a happy thing to say.

'It's the sort of thing that happens,' he said. 'It's . . . er . . . magic.'

'Oh. Really? Oh.'

A cup bumped gently off Carrot's ear. He batted it away and it disappeared somewhere aft.

'What *kind* of magic?' he said.

he wizards were clustered around the piece of omniscope, while Ponder struggled to adjust it.

A picture exploded into view. It was horrible.

'Hello? Hello? This is Ankh-Morpork calling!'

The gibbering face was pushed aside and Leonard's dome rose slowly into view.

'Ah, yes. Good morning,' he said. 'We are having a few . . . teething troubles.'

From somewhere offscreen came the sound of someone being sick.

'*What is going on?*' bellowed Ridcully.

'Well, you see, it's rather amusing . . . I had this idea of putting food in tubes, you see, so that it could be squeezed out and eaten neatly in weightless conditions and, er, because we didn't tie *everything* down, er, I'm afraid my box of paints came open and the tubes got, er, confused, so what Mr Rincewind thought was broccoli and ham turned out to be Forest Green . . . er.'

'Let me speak to Captain Carrot, will you?'

'I'm afraid that is not entirely convenient at the moment,' said Leonard, his face clouded with concern.

'Why? Did he have the broccoli and ham too?'

'No, he had the Cadmium Yellow.' There was a yelp and a series of clangs somewhere behind Leonard. 'On the brighter side, however, I can report that the Mk II privy appears to function *perfectly*.'

he *Kite*, in its headlong plunge, curved back towards the Rimfall. Now the water was a great tumbling cloud of mist.

Captain Carrot hovered in front of a window, taking pictures with the iconograph.

'This is *amazing*,' he said. 'I'm sure we'll find the answers to some questions that have puzzled mankind for millennia.'

'Good. Can you get this frying pan off my back?' said Rincewind.

'Um,' said Leonard.

It was a sufficiently troubling syllable for the others to look at him.

'We seem to be, er, losing air rather faster than I thought,' said the genius. 'But I'm *sure* the hull isn't any leakier than I allowed for. And we seem to be falling faster, according to Mr Stibbons. Uh . . . it's a little difficult to piece it all together, of course, because of the uncertain effects of the Disc's magical field. Um . . . we should be all right if we wear our helmets all the time . . . '

'There's plenty of air nearer to the world, isn't there?' said Rincewind. 'Can't we just fly into it and open a window?'

Leonard stared mournfully into the mists that filled half of their view.

'We are, er, moving very fast,' he said, slowly. 'And air at this speed . . . air is . . . the thing about air . . . tell me, what do you understand by the words "shooting star"?'

'What is that supposed to mean?' Rincewind demanded.

'Um . . . that we die an immensely horrible death.'

'Oh, *that*,' said Rincewind.

Leonard tapped a dial on one of the tanks of air. 'I really don't think my calculations were that wro—'

Light exploded into the cabin.

The *Kite* rose through tendrils of mist.

The crew stared.

'No one will ever believe us,' said Carrot, eventually. He raised his iconograph towards the view and even the imp inside, which belonged to a species that was seldom impressed with anything, said 'Gosh!' in a tiny voice as it painted furiously.

'I don't believe this,' said Rincewind, 'and I'm *seeing* it.'

A tower, an immensity of rock, rose from the mist. And looming over the mist, huge as worlds, the backs of four elephants. It was like flying through a cathedral, thousands of miles high.

'It sounds like a joke,' Rincewind babbled, 'elephants holding up the world, hahaha . . . and then you see it . . . '

'My paints, where are my *paints* . . . ?' mumbled Leonard.

'Well, some of them are in the privy,' said Rincewind.

Carrot turned, and looked puzzled. The iconograph floated away, trailing small curses.

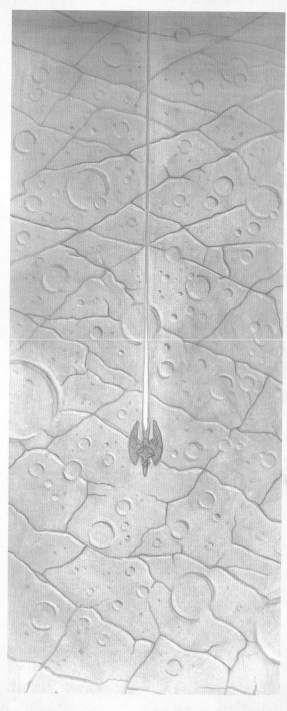

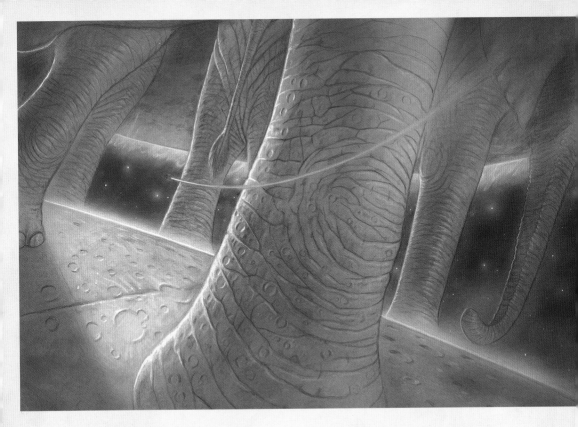

'And where's my apple?' he said.

'What?' said Rincewind, perplexed at the sudden subject of fruit.

'I'd just started eating an apple, and I just rested it in the air . . . and it's *gone*.'

The ship creaked in the glaring sunlight.

And an apple core came tumbling gently through the air.

'I suppose there *are* just the three of us aboard?' said Rincewind innocently.

'Don't be silly,' said Carrot. 'We're sealed in!'

'So . . . your apple ate itself?'

They looked at the jumble of bundles held in the webbing behind them.

'I mean, call me Mr Suspicious,' said Rincewind, 'but if the ship is *heavier* than Leonard thought, and we're using up more air, and food is vanishing—'

'You're not suggesting that there's some kind of monster floating around below the Rim that can bore into wooden hulls, are you?' said Carrot, drawing his sword.

'Ah, I hadn't thought of *that* one,' said Rincewind. 'Well done.'

'Interesting,' said Leonard. 'It would be, perhaps, a cross between a bird and a bivalve. Somewhat squid-like, possibly, using jets of—'

'Thank you, thank you, thank you, yes!'

Carrot pulled out a roll of blankets and tried to look back along the cabin.

'I think I saw something move,' he said. 'Just behind the air reservoirs . . .'

He ducked under a bundle of skis and disappeared into the shadows.

They heard him groan.

'Oh, no . . .'

'What? What?' said Rincewind.

Carrot's voice was muffled. 'I've found a . . . it looks like a . . . skin . . .'

'Ah, fascinating,' said Leonard, sketching on his notepad. 'Possibly, once aboard a hospitable vessel, such a creature would metamorphose into—'

Carrot emerged, a banana skin kebabed on the end of his sword.

Rincewind rolled his eyes. 'I have a very definite feeling about this,' he said.

'So have I,' said Carrot.

It took them some time, but finally they pushed away a box of dishcloths and there were no more hiding places.

A worried face looked out of the nest it had made.

'Ook?' it said.

Leonard sighed, laid aside his pad and opened up the omniscope's box. He banged on it once or twice, and it flickered and showed the outline of a head.

Leonard took a deep breath.

'Ankh-Morpork, we have an orangutan . . .'

ohen sheathed his sword.

'Wouldn't have expected much to be living up here,' he said, surveying the carnage.

'There's even less now,' said Caleb.

The latest fight had been over in the twinkling of an eye and the cleaving of a backbone. Any . . . creatures that ambushed the Horde did so at the *end* of their lives.

'The raw magic here must be huge,' said Boy Willie. 'I suppose creatures like this get used to living off it. Sooner or later something will learn to live *anywhere*.'

'It's certainly doing Mad Hamish good,' said Cohen. 'I'll swear he's not as deaf as he was.'

'Whut?'

'I SAID YOU'RE NOT AS DEAF AS YOU WERE, HAMISH!'

'There's no need to shout, mon!'

'Can we cook 'em, do you think?' said Boy Willie.

'They'll probably taste a bit like chicken,' said Caleb. 'Everything does, if you're hungry enough.'

'Leave it to me,' said Mrs McGarry. 'You get a fire going, and I'll make this taste more like chicken than . . . chicken.'

Cohen wandered off to where the minstrel was sitting by himself, working on the remains of his lute. The lad had brightened up considerably as the climb progressed, Cohen thought. He had completely stopped whimpering.

Cohen sat down next to him.

'What're you doing, lad?' he said. 'I see you found a skull.'

'It's going to be the sound box,' said the minstrel. He looked worried for a moment. 'That *is* all right, isn't it?'

'Sure. Good fate for a hero, having his bones made into a harp or something. It should sing out wonderful.'

'This will be a kind of lyre,' said the minstrel. 'It's going to be a bit primitive, I'm afraid.'

'Even better. Good for the old songs,' said Cohen.

'I have been thinking about the . . . the saga,' the minstrel admitted.

'Good lad, good lad. Plenty of spakes?'

'Um, yes. But I thought I'd start off with the legend of how Mazda stole fire for mankind in the first place.'

'Nice,' said Cohen.

'And then a few verses about what the gods did to him,' the minstrel went on, tightening a string.

'Did to him? Did to him?' said Cohen. 'They made him immortal!'

'Er . . . yes. In a *way*, I suppose.'

'What do you mean, "in a way"?'

'It's classical mythology, Cohen,' said the minstrel. 'I thought everyone knew. He was chained to a rock for eternity and every day an eagle comes and pecks out his liver.'

'Is that true?'

'It's mentioned in many of the classic texts.'

'I'm not much of a reader,' said Cohen. 'Chained to a rock? For a first offence? He's still there?'

'Eternity isn't finished yet, Cohen.'

'He must've had a big liver!'

'It grows again every night, according to the legend,' said the minstrel.

'I wish my kidneys did,' said Cohen. He stared at the distant clouds that hid the snowy top of the mountain. 'He brought fire to everyone, and the gods did that to him, eh? Well . . . we'll have to see about that.'

he omniscope showed a snowstorm.

'Bad weather down there, then,' said Ridcully.

'No, it's thaumic interference,' said Ponder. 'They're passing under the elephants. We'll get a lot more of it, I'm afraid.'

'Did they *really* say "Ankh-Morpork, we have an orangutan"?' said the Dean.

'The Librarian must have got on board somehow,' said Ponder. 'You know what he's like for finding odd corners to sleep in. And that, I'm afraid, explains the weight and the air. Er . . . I have to tell you that I'm not sure that they have enough time or power to get back on to the Disc now.'

'What do you mean, you're *not sure*?' said Lord Vetinari.

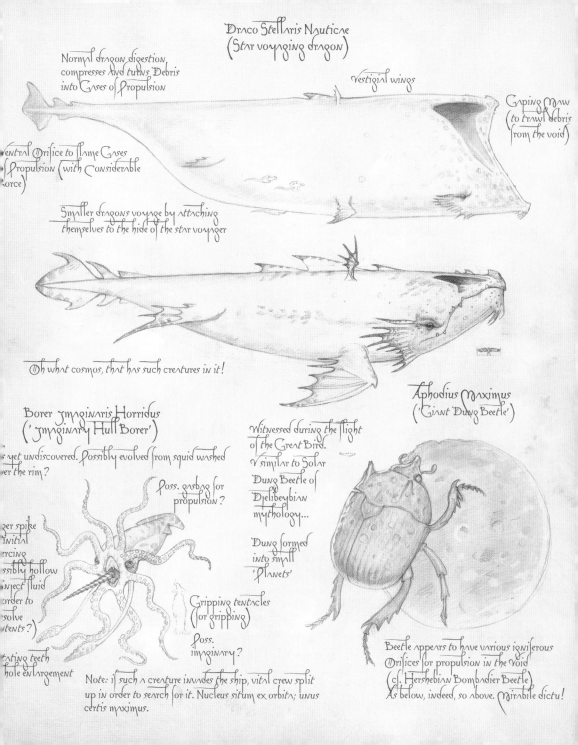

Draco Stellaris Nauticae
(Star voyaging dragon)

Normal dragon digestion compresses and turns Debris into Gases of Propulsion

Vestigial wings

Gaping Maw (to trawl debris from the void)

Ventral Orifice to flame Gases of Propulsion (with Considerable Force)

Smaller dragons voyage by attaching themselves to the hide of the star voyager

Oh what cosmos, that has such creatures in it!

Borer Imaginaris Horridus
('Imaginary Hull Borer')

As yet undiscovered. Possibly evolved from squid washed over the rim?

Poss. gasbag for propulsion?

Borer spike (initial piercing possibly hollow to inject fluid in order to dissolve contents?)

Rotating teeth for hole enlargement

Gripping tentacles (for gripping)

Poss. imaginary?

Note: if such a creature invades the ship, vital crew split up in order to search for it. Nucleus situm ex orbita; unus certis maximus.

Aphodius Maximus
('Giant Dung Beetle')

Witnessed during the flight of the Great Bird. Similar to Solar Dung Beetle of Djelibeybian mythology...

Dung formed into small 'Planets'

Beetle appears to have various igniferous Orifices for propulsion in the Void (cf. Hershebian Bombadier Beetle) As below, indeed, so above. Mirabile dictu!

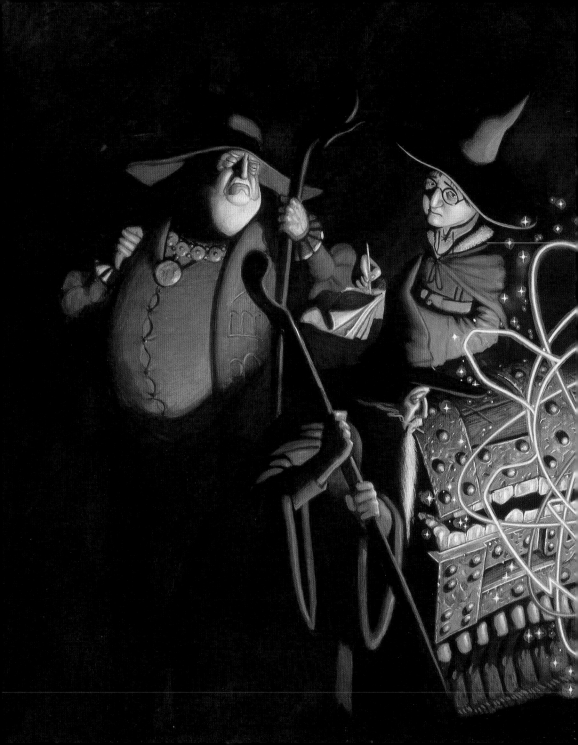

'Er . . . I mean I *am* sure but, er, no one likes bad news all at once, sir.'

Lord Vetinari looked at the big spell that dominated the cabin. It floated in the air: the whole world, sketched in glowing lines and, dropping from one glittering edge, a small curving line. As he watched it lengthened slightly.

'They can't just turn around and come back?' he said.

'No, sir. It doesn't work like that.'

'Can they throw the Librarian out?'

The wizards looked shocked.

'*No*, sir,' said Ponder. 'That would be murder, sir.'

'Yes, but they may save the world. One ape dies, one world lives. You do not need to be a rocket wizard to work that out, surely?'

'You can't ask them to make a decision like that, sir!'

'Really? I make decisions like that every day,' said Lord Vetinari. 'Oh, very well. What are they short of?'

'Air and dragon power, sir.'

'If they chop up the orangutan and feed him to the dragons, won't that kill two birds with one stone?'

The sudden iciness told Lord Vetinari that once again he hadn't taken his audience with him. He sighed.

'They need dragon flame to . . . ?' he said.

'To bring their ringpath over the Disc, sir. They have to fire the dragons at the right time.'

Vetinari looked at the magical orrery again. 'And now . . . ?'

'I'm not quite sure, sir. They may crash into the Disc, or they may shoot straight out into endless space.'

'And they need air . . . '

'Yes, sir.'

Vetinari's arm moved through the outline of the world and a long forefinger pointed.

'Is there any air *here*?' he said.

'hat meal,' said Cohen, 'was heroic. No other word for it.'

'That's right, Mrs McGarry,' said Evil Harry. 'Even rat doesn't taste this much like chicken.'

'Yes, the tentacles hardly spoiled it at all!' said Caleb enthusiastically.

They sat and watched the view. What had once been the world below was now a world in front, rising like an endless wall.

'What're they, right up there?' said Cohen, pointing.

'Thanks, friend,' said Evil Harry, looking away. 'I'd like the . . . chicken to stay down, if it's all the same to you.'

'They're the Virgin Islands,' said the minstrel. 'So called because there's so many of them.'

'Or maybe they're hard to find,' said Truckle the Uncivil, burping. 'Hur, hur, hur.'

'Ye can see the stars from up here,' said Mad Hamish, 'e'en though 'tis day.'

Cohen grinned at him. It wasn't often Mad Hamish volunteered anything.

'They say every one of 'em's a world,' said Evil Harry.

'Yeah,' said Cohen. 'How many, bard?'

'I don't know. Thousands. Millions,' said the minstrel.

'Millions of worlds, and *we* get . . . what? How old are you, Hamish?'

'Whut? I were born the day the old thane died,' said Hamish.

'When was that? Which old thane?' said Cohen patiently.

'Whut? I ain't a scholar! I canna remember that kinda stuff!'

'A hundred years, maybe,' said Cohen. 'One hundred years. And there's millions o' worlds.' He took a pull of his cigarette and rubbed his forehead with the back of his thumb. 'It's a bugger.'

He nodded at the minstrel. 'What did your mate Carelinus do after he'd blown his nose?'

'Look, you really shouldn't think of him like that,' said the minstrel hotly. 'He built a huge empire . . . too big, really. And in many ways he was a lot like you. Haven't you heard of the Tsortean Knot?'

'Sounds dirty,' said Truckle. 'Hur, hur, hur . . . sorry.'

The minstrel sighed. 'It was a huge, complicated knot that tied two beams together in the Temple of Offler in Tsort, and it was said that whoever untied it would reign over the whole of the continent,' he said.

'They can be very tricky, knots,' said Mrs McGarry.

'Carelinus sliced right through it with his sword!' said the minstrel. The revelation of this dramatic gesture did not get the applause he expected.

'So he was a cheat as well as a cry-baby?' said Boy Willie.

'No! It was a dramatic, nay, portentous gesture!' snapped the minstrel.

'Yeah, okay, but it's not exactly *untying* it, is it? I mean, if the rules said "untying", I don't see why he should—'

'Nah, nah, the lad's got a point,' said Cohen, who seemed to have been turning this one over in his mind. 'It wasn't cheating, because it was a good story. Yeah. I can understand that.' He chuckled. 'I can just imagine it, too. A load of whey-faced priests and suchlike standin' around and thinkin', "that's *cheatin*', but he's got a really *big* sword so I won't be the first to point this out, plus this damn great army is just outside". Hah. Yeah. Hmm. What did he do next?'

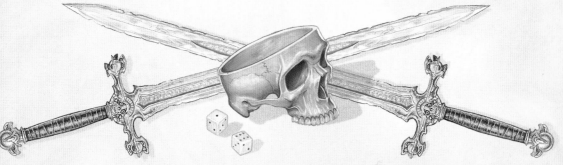

'Conquered most of the known world.'

'Good lad. And after that?'

'He . . . er . . . went home, reigned for a few years, then he died and his sons squabbled and there were a few wars . . . and that was the end of the empire.'

'Children can be a problem,' said Vena, without looking up from carefully embroidering forget-me-nots around BURN THIS HOUSE.

'Some people say you achieve immortality through your children,' said the minstrel.

'Yeah?' said Cohen. 'Name one of your great-granddads, then.'

'Well . . . er . . .'

'See? Now, I got lots of kids,' said Cohen. 'Haven't seen most of 'em . . . you know how it is. But they had fine strong mothers and I hope like hell they're all living for themselves, not for me. Fat lot of good they did your Carelinus, losin' his empire for him.'

'But there's lots more a proper historian could tell you—' said the minstrel.

'Hah!' said Cohen. 'It's what ordin'ry people remember that matters. It's songs and sayin's. It doesn't matter how you live and die, it's how the bards wrote it down.'

The minstrel felt their joint gaze fix on him.

'Um . . . I'm making *lots* of notes,' he said.

‘Ook,' said the Librarian, by way of explanation.

'And then he says something fell on his head,' Rincewind translated. 'It must have been when we dived.'

'Can we throw some of this stuff out of the ship to lighten it?' said Carrot. 'We don't need most of it.'

'Alas, no,' said Leonard. 'We will lose all our air if we open the door.'

'But we've got these breathing helmets,' Rincewind pointed out.

'*Three* helmets,' said Leonard.

The omniscope crackled. They ignored it. The *Kite* was still passing under the elephants, and the thing showed mostly a kind of magical snow.

But Rincewind did glance up, and saw that someone in the storm was holding a card on which had been scrawled, in large letters: STAND BY.

Ponder shook his head.

'Thank you, Archchancellor, but I'm far too busy for you to help me,' he said.

'But will it work?'

'It has to, sir. It's a million-to-one chance.'

'Oh, then we don't have to worry. Everyone knows million-to-one chances always work.'

'Yes, sir. So all I have to do is work out if there's still enough air outside the ship for Leonard to steer it, or how many dragons he will need to fire for how long, and if there will be enough power left to get them off again. I *think* he's travelling at nearly the right speed, but I'm not sure how much flame the dragons will have left, and I don't know what kind of

Clothing of the Empty Void

mk 1.0 Rincewind

Converted pearl Diving Helmet with Simple Pressure Gauge (if eyeholes turn red, head has exploded).

Light boots for moving fast in the event of Unexpectedness.

Oiled leather suit over canvas undersuit over three layers of wool for warmth in the Endless Gulfs.

Pocket (special order from crew member) containing cards with messages such as 'Run!', 'I surrender!', 'Stercus', 'Help!' and so on, for use in the Soundless Spaces. There can be no voice where there is no motion or percussion of the air.

Capacious thigh pouches for collecting e.g. rocks (and also to combat excessive Levity).

Pocket for Handkerchief.

Adorno maximus, magister!

mk 3.0 Leonard of Quirm

Blown glass helmet for All-round Observation.

Improved Air Renewer.

Pockets to hold pencils, crayons, notebooks etc.

Emergency air supply in puffed sleeves.

Holster for brushes.

Weighted boots to hold wearer down e.g. in conditions of Levity.

Experimental 'recycling' pants (alas, not quite perfect yet).

mk 2.0 Captain Carrot (Warrior)

Lightweight suit of stretched leather and canvas.

Light leather gloves with mail outer covering.

Heavy leather bands to prevent chest exploding.

Adapted traditional helmet.

surface he'll land on or anything they'll find there. I can adapt a few spells, but they were never devised for this sort of thing.'

'Good man,' said Ridcully.

'Is there anything we can do to help?' said the Dean.

Ponder gave the other wizards a desperate look. How would Lord Vetinari have handled this?

'Why, yes,' he said brightly. 'Perhaps you would be kind enough to find a cabin somewhere and come up with a list of all the various ways I could solve this? And I will just sit here and toy with a few ideas?'

'That's what I like to see,' said the Dean. 'A lad with enough sense to make use of the wisdom of his elders.'

Lord Vetinari gave Ponder a faint smile as they left the cabin.

In the sudden silence Ponder . . . pondered. He stared at the orrery, walked around it, enlarged sections of it, peered at them, pored over the notes he had made about the power of dragon flight, stared at a model of the *Kite*, and spent a lot of time looking at the ceiling.

This wasn't the normal way of working for a wizard. A wizard evolved the wish, and then devised the command. He didn't bother much with observing the universe; rocks and trees and clouds could not have anything very intelligent to impart. They didn't even have writing on them, after all.

Ponder looked at the numbers he had scribbled. As a calculation, it was like balancing a feather on a soap bubble which wasn't there.

So he guessed.

n the *Kite*, the situation was being 'workshopped'. This is the means by which people who don't know anything get together to pool their ignorance.

'Could we all hold our breath for a quarter of the time?' said Carrot.

'No. Breath doesn't work like that, alas,' said Leonard.

'Perhaps we should all stop talking?' said Rincewind.

'Ook,' said the Librarian, pointing to the fuzzy screen of the omniscope.

Someone was holding up another placard. The huge words could just be made out: THIS IS WHAT YOU DO.

Leonard snatched a pencil and began to scribble in the corner of a drawing of a machine for undermining city walls.

Five minutes later he put it down again.

'Remarkable,' he said. 'He wants us to point the *Kite* in a different direction and go faster.'

'Where to?'

'He doesn't say. But . . . ah, yes. He wants us to fly directly towards the sun.'

Leonard gave them one of his bright smiles. It faced three blank stares.

'It will mean allowing one or two individual dragons to flare for a few seconds, to bring us around, and then—'

'The sun,' said Rincewind.

'It's *hot*,' said Carrot.

'Yes, and I am sure we're all very glad of that,' said Leonard, unrolling a plan of the *Kite*.

'Ook!'

'I'm sorry?'

'He said, "And this boat is made of wood!"' said Rincewind.

'All that in one syllable?'

'He's a very concise thinker! Look, Stibbons must have made a mistake. I wouldn't trust a wizard to give me directions to the other side of a very small room!'

'He does seem to be a bright young man, though,' said Carrot.

'You'll be bright, too, if you're in this thing when it hits the sun,' said Rincewind. 'Incandescent, I expect.'

'We *can* point the *Kite*, if we're very careful how we operate the port and starboard mirrors,' said Leonard thoughtfully. 'There may be a little trial and error . . .'

'Ah, we seem to have the hang of it, ' said Leonard. He turned over a small eggtimer.

'And now, all dragons for two minutes . . .'

'I ssuppose he'll ttell uss ssoon wwhat happens nnext?' shouted Carrot, while behind them things tinkled and creaked.

'Mmr Sstibbonss hhas ttwo ththousand yyears of uuniversity eexpertise bbehind hhim!' yelled Leonard, above the din.

'Hhow mmuch of ththat hhas iinvolved ssteering fflying sships wwith ddragons?' screamed Rincewind.

Leonard leaned against the tug of home-made gravity and looked at the eggtimer.

'Aabout wwwwwone hhundred sseconds!'

'Ah! Iiit'ss ppractically aaa ttradition, tthenn!'

Erratically, the dragons stopped flaming. Once again, things filled the air.

And there was the sun. But no longer circular. Something had clipped its edge.

'Ah,' said Leonard. 'How clever. Gentlemen, behold the moon!'

'We're going to hit the moon instead?' said Carrot. 'Is that *better*?'

'My feelings exactly,' said Rincewind.

'Ook!'

'I don't think we're going so very fast,' said Leonard. 'We're only just catching it up. I think Mr Stibbons intends that we *land* on it.'

He flexed his fingers.

'There's some air there, I'm sure of it,' he went on. 'Which means there is probably something we can feed to the dragons. And then, and this is very clever thinking, we ride on the moon until it rises over the Disc, and all we need to do is drop down lightly.'

He kicked the release on the wing levers. The cabin rattled to the spinning of the flywheels. On either side, the *Kite* spread its wings.

'Any questions?' he said.

'I'm trying to think of all the things that could go wrong,' said Carrot.

'I've got to nine so far,' said Rincewind. 'And I haven't *started* on the fine detail.'

The moon *was* getting bigger, a dark sphere eclipsing the light of the distant sun.

'As I understand it,' said Leonard, as it began to loom in the windows, 'the moon, being much smaller and lighter than the Disc, can only hold on to light things, like air. Heavier things, like the *Kite*, should hardly be able to stay on the ground.'

'And that means . . . ?' said Carrot.

'Er . . . we should just *float* down,' said Leonard. 'But holding on to something *might* be a good idea . . . '

They landed. It's a short sentence, but contains a lot of incident.

here was silence on the boat, apart from the sound of the sea and Ponder Stibbons's urgent muttering as he tried to adjust the omniscope.

'The screams . . .' murmured Mustrum Ridcully, after a while.

'But then they screamed a second time, a few seconds later,' said Lord Vetinari.

'And a few seconds after *that*,' said the Dean.

'I thought the omniscope could see *anywhere*,' said the Patrician, watching the sweat pour off Ponder.

'The shards, er, don't seem stable when they're too far apart, sir,' said Ponder. 'Uh . . . and there's still a couple of thousand miles of world and elephant between them . . . ah . . . ' The omniscope flickered, and then went blank again.

'A good wizard, Rincewind,' said the Chair of Indefinite Studies. 'Not particularly bright, but, frankly, I've never been quite happy with intelligence. An overrated talent, in my humble opinion.'

Ponder's ears went red.

'Perhaps we should put a small plaque up somewhere in the University,' said Ridcully. 'Nothing garish, of course.'

'Gentlemen, are you forgetting?' said Lord Vetinari. 'Soon there will *be* no University.'

'Ah. Well, a small saving there, then.'

'*Hello? Hello? Is there anyone there?*'

And there was, fuzzy but recognisable, a face peering out of the omniscope.

'Captain Carrot?' Ridcully roared. 'How did you get that damn thing to work?'

'*I just stopped sitting on it, sir.*'

'Are you all right? We heard screams!' said Ponder.

'*That was when we hit the ground, sir.*'

'But then we heard screams *again*.'

'*That was probably when we hit the ground for the second time, sir.*'

'And the third time?'

'*Ground again, sir. You could say the landing was a bit . . . tentative . . . for a while there.*'

Lord Vetinari leaned forward. 'Where are you?'

'*Here, sir. On the moon. Mr Stibbons was right. There is air here. It's a bit thin, but it's fine if your plans for the day include breathing.*'

'Mr Stibbons was right, was he?' said Ridcully, staring at Ponder. 'How did you work that out so *exactly*, Mr Stibbons?'

'I, er . . . ' Ponder felt the eyes of the wizards on him. 'I—' He stopped. 'It was a lucky guess, sir.'

The wizards relaxed. They were extremely uneasy with cleverness, but lucky guessing was what being a wizard was all about.

'Well done, that man,' said Ridcully, nodding. 'Wipe your forehead, Mr Stibbons, you've got away with it again.'

'*I've taken the liberty of asking Rincewind to take a picture of me planting the flag of Ankh-Morpork and claiming the moon on behalf of all the nations of the Disc, your lordship,*' Carrot went on.

'Very . . . patriotic,' said Lord Vetinari. 'I may even tell them.'

'*However, I can't show you this on the omniscope because, shortly afterwards, something ate the flag. Things here . . . aren't entirely what you'd expect, sir.*'

They were definitely dragons. Rincewind could see that. But they resembled swamp dragons in the same way that greyhounds resembled those odd yappy little dogs with lots of Zs and Xs in their name.

They were all nose and sleek body, with longer arms and legs than the swamp variety, and they were so silvery that they looked like moonlight hammered into shape.

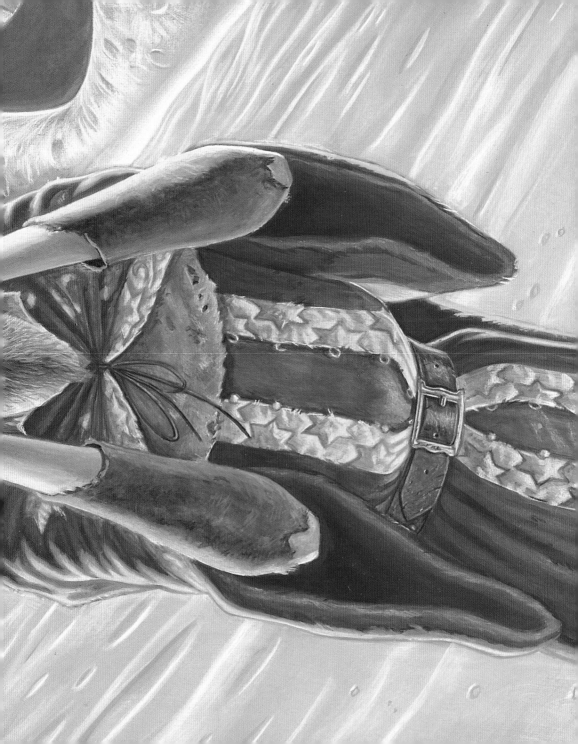

And . . . they flamed. But it was not from the end that Rincewind had, hitherto, associated with dragons.

The strange thing was, as Leonard said, that once you stopped sniggering about the whole idea it made a lot of sense. It was so stupid for a flying creature to have a weapon which stopped it dead in midair, for example.

Dragons of all sizes surrounded the *Kite*, watching it with deer-like curiosity. Occasionally one or two would leap into the air and roar away, but others would land to join the throng. They stared at the crew of the *Kite* as if they were expecting them to do tricks, or make an important announcement.

There was greenery, too, except that it was silvery. Lunar vegetation covered most of the surface. The *Kite*'s third bounce and long slide had left a trail through it. The leaves were—

'Hold still, will you?' Rincewind's attention was drawn to his patient as the Librarian struggled; the problem with bandaging an orangutan's head is knowing when to stop. 'It's your own fault,' he said. 'I *told* you. Small steps, I said. Not giant leaps.'

Carrot and Leonard bounced around the side of the *Kite*.

'Hardly any damage at all,' said the inventor as he drifted down. 'The whole thing took the shock remarkably well. And we're pointing slightly upwards. In this . . . general lightness, that should be quite sufficient to allow us to take off again, although there is one minor problem— Shoo, will you?'

He waved away a small silver dragon that was sniffing at the *Kite*, and it took off vertically on a needle of blue flame.

'We're out of food for our dragons,' said Rincewind. 'I've looked. The fuel bunker broke open when we landed for the first time.'

Some observations upon 'Moon Dragons'

Wings: small, ornamental

Beard and thrips: luxuriant, swept back

Squales: enlarged, prominent, poss. for steering?

Body shape: sleek

Posture: regal, alert

Young moon dragons. Note elevation of the quenzals and early growth of thrips. The one of the left is noticeably hammeling.

Egg: curiously shaped, possibly to survive long drop to the ground

'But we can feed them some of the silver plants, can't we?' said Carrot. 'The ones here seem to do very well on them.'

'Aren't they *magnificent* creatures?' said Leonard as a squadron of the creatures sailed overhead.

They turned to watch the flight, and then stared beyond it. There was possibly no limit to how often the view could amaze you.

The moon was rising over the world, and elephant's head filled half the sky.

It was . . . simply big. Too big to describe.

Wordlessly, all four voyagers climbed a small mound to get a clear view, and they stood in silence for some time. Dark eyes the size of oceans stared at them. Great crescents of ivory obscured the stars.

There was no sound but the occasional click and swish as the iconograph imp painted picture after picture.

Space wasn't big. It wasn't there. It was just nothing and therefore, in Rincewind's view, nothing to get humble about. But the *world* was big, and the elephant was *huge*.

130

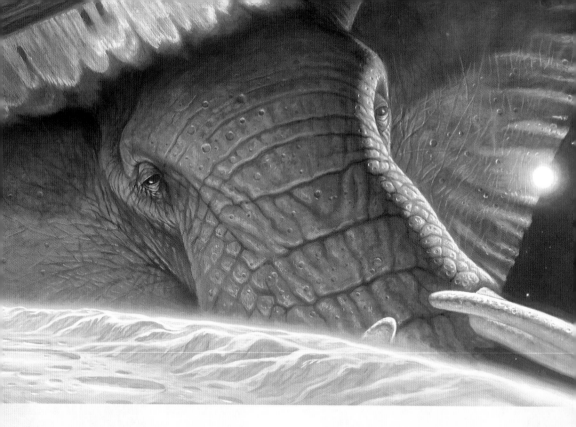

'Which one is it?' said Leonard, after a while.

'I don't know,' said Carrot. 'You know, I'm not sure I ever really believed it before. You know . . . about the turtle and the elephants and everything. Seeing it all like this makes me feel very . . . very . . . '

'Scared?' suggested Rincewind.

'No.'

'Upset?'

'No.'

'Easily intimidated?'

'No.'

Beyond the Rimfall, the continents of the world were coming into view under swirls of white cloud.

'You know . . . from up here . . . you can't see the boundaries between nations,' said Carrot, almost wistfully.

'Is that a problem?' said Leonard. 'Possibly something could be done.'

131

'Maybe huge, really *huge* buildings in lines, along the frontiers,' said Rincewind. 'Or . . . or very wide roads. You could paint them different colours to save confusion.'

'Should aerial travel become widespread,' said Leonard, 'it would be a useful idea to grow forests in the shape of the name of the country, or of other areas of note. I will bear this in mind.'

'I wasn't actually *sugges*—' Carrot began. And then he stopped, and just sighed.

They went on watching, unable to tear themselves away from the view. Tiny sparkles in the sky showed where more flocks of dragons were sweeping between the world and the moon.

'We never see them back home,' said Rincewind.

'I suspect the swamp dragons are their descendants, poor little things,' said Leonard. 'Adapted for heavy air.'

'I wonder what else lives down here that we don't know about?' said Carrot.

'Well, there's always the invisible squid-like creature that sucks all the air out of—' Rincewind began, but sarcasm did not carry very well out here. The universe diluted it. The huge, black, solemn eyes in the sky withered it.

Besides, there was just . . . *too much*. Too much of everything. He wasn't used to seeing this much universe all in one go. The blue disc of the world, unrolling slowly as the moon rose, looked outnumbered.

'It's all too big,' said Rincewind.

'Yes.'

'Ook.'

There was nothing to do but wait for full moonrise. Or Discsink.

Carrot carefully lifted a small dragon out of a coffee cup. 'The little ones get everywhere,' he said. 'Just like kittens. But the adults just keep their distance and stare at us.'

'Like cats, then,' said Rincewind. He lifted up his hat and untangled a small silvery dragon from his hair.

'I wonder if we ought to take a few back?'

'We'll be taking them *all* back if we're not careful!'

'They look a bit like Errol,' said Carrot. 'You know, the little dragon that was our Watch mascot? He saved the city by working out how to, er, flame backwards. We all thought he was some new kind of dragon,' Carrot added, 'but now it looks as though he was a throwback. Is Leonard still out there?'

They looked out at Leonard, who had taken half an hour off to do some painting. A small dragon had perched on his shoulder.

'He says he's never seen light like it,' said Rincewind. 'He says he *must* have a picture. He's doing very well, considering.'

'Considering what?'

'Considering that two of the tubes he was using contain tomato purée and cream cheese.'

'Did you tell him?'

'I didn't like to. He was so enthusiastic.'

'We'd better start feeding the dragons,' said Carrot, putting his cup down.

'All right. Can you unstick this frying pan from my head, please?'

Half an hour later the flicker of the omniscope screen illuminated Ponder's cabin.

'*We've fed the dragons,*' said Carrot. '*The plants here are . . . odd. They seem to be made of a sort of glassy metal. Leonard has a rather impressive theory that they absorb sunlight during the day and then shine at night, thus creating "moonlight". The dragons seem to find it very tasty. Anyway, we shall be leaving shortly. I am just collecting some rocks.*'

'I'm sure they will come in useful,' said Lord Vetinari.

'Actually, sir, they will be very valuable,' whispered Ponder Stibbons.

'Really?' said the Patrician.

'Oh, yes! They may well be completely different from rocks on the Disc!'

'And if they are exactly the same?'

'Oh, *that* would be even *more* interesting, sir!'

Lord Vetinari looked at Ponder without speaking. He could deal with most types of mind, but the one apparently operating Ponder Stibbons was of a sort he had yet to find the handles on. It was best to nod and smile and give it the bits of machinery it seemed to think were so important, lest it run amok.

'Well done,' he said. 'Ah, yes, of course . . . and the rocks may contain valuable ores, or possibly even diamonds?'

Ponder shrugged. 'I wouldn't know about that, sir. But they may tell us more about the history of the moon.'

Vetinari's brow wrinkled. '*History?*' he said. 'But no one *lives* th— I mean, yes, well done. Tell me, do you have all the machinery you need?'

The swamp dragons chewed at the moon leaves. They *were* metallic, with a glassy surface, and little blue and green sparks sizzled over the dragons' teeth when they bit into them. The voyagers piled them up high in front of the cages.

Unfortunately, the only explorer who would have noticed that the moon dragons ate only the occasional leaf was Leonard, and he had been too busy painting.

Swamp dragons, on the other hand, were used to eating a *lot* of things in the energy-poor environment of their world.

Stomachs used to transmuting the equivalent of stale cakes into usable flame took delivery of dialectric surfaces chock-full of almost pure energy. It was the food of the gods.

It was only going to be a matter of time before one of them burped.

The whole of the Disc was . . . well, there was the problem, from Rincewind's point of view. It was *below* them now. It *looked* below, even if it was really just *over there*. He couldn't get over the dreadful feeling that once the *Kite* was airborne it would simply drop down to those distant, fleecy clouds.

The Librarian helped him winch in the wing on his side, as Leonard made ready to depart.

'Well, I mean, I *know* we've got wings and everything,' Rincewind said. 'It's just that I'm not at home in an environment where every direction is down.'

'Ook.'

'I don't *know* what I'll say to him. "Don't blow the world up" sounds a pretty persuasive argument to me. *I'd* listen to it. And I don't like the idea of going *anywhere* near the gods. We're like toys to them, you know.' *And they don't realise how easily the arms and legs come off,* he added to himself.

'Ook?'

'Pardon? Do you *really* say that?'

'Ook.'

'There is a . . . *monkey* god?'

'Ook?'

'No, no, that's fine, fine. Not one of our locals ones, is he?'

'Eek.'

'Oh, the Counterweight Continent. Well, they'll believe just about anything over . . .' He glanced out of the window and shuddered, '*Down* there.'

There was a thud as the ratchet clicked into place.

'Thank you, gentlemen,' said Leonard. 'Now if you'll just take your seats we—'

The thump of an explosion rocked the *Kite* and knocked Rincewind off his feet.

'How curious, one of the dragons appears to have fired a little earl—'

'ehold!' said Cohen, striking a pose.

The Silver Horde looked around.

'What?' said Evil Harry.

'*Behold*, the citadels of the gods!' said Cohen, striking the pose again.

'Yes, well, we can see it,' said Caleb. 'Is there something wrong with your back?'

'Write down that I spake "Behold!",' said Cohen to the minstrel. 'You don't have to write down any of this other stuff.'

'You wouldn't mind saying—'

'—spaking—'

'—sorry, *spaking*, "Behold the temples of the gods", would you?' said the minstrel. 'It's got a better rhythm.'

'Hah, this takes me back,' said Truckle. 'Remember, Hamish? You and me signed on with Duke Leofric the Legitimate when he invaded Nothingfjord?'

'Aye, I mind it.'

'Five damn days, that battle took,' said Truckle, ''cos the Duchess was doing a tapestry to commemorate it, right? We had to keep doing the fights over and over again, and there was the devil to pay when she was changing needles. There's no place for the media on the field of battle, I've always said.'

'Aye, and I mind you makin' a rude sign to the ladies!' Hamish cackled. 'I saw that ol' tapestry in the castle of Rosante years later and I could tell it wuz you!'

'Could we just get on with it?' said Vena.

'Y'see, there's the problem,' said Cohen. 'It's no good *just* doin' it. You got to remember your posterity.'

'Hur, hur, hur,' said Truckle.

'Laugh away,' said Cohen. 'But what about all those heroes that aren't remembered in songs and sagas, eh? You tell me about *them*.'

'Eh? *What* heroes that aren't remembered in songs and sagas?'

'*Exactly!*'

'What's the plan?' said Evil Harry, who had been watching the shimmering light over the city of the gods.

'Plan?' said Cohen. 'I thought you knew. We're going to sneak in, smash the igniter, and run like hell.'

'Yes, but how do you *plan* to do this?' said Evil Harry. He sighed when he saw their faces. 'You haven't got one, have you?' he said wearily. 'You were just going to rush in, weren't you? Heroes *never* have a plan. It's always left up to us Dark Lords to have the plans. This is the home of the *gods*, lads! You think they won't notice a bunch of humans wandering around?'

'We *are* intendin' to have a magnificent death,' said Cohen.

'Right, right. *Afterwards*. Oh, deary me. Look, I'd be thrown out of the secret society of evil madmen if I let you go at it mob-handed.' Evil Harry shook his head. 'There's hundreds

of gods, right? Everyone knows that. And new gods turning up all the time, right? Well? Doesn't a plan suggest itself? Anyone?'

Truckle raised a hand. 'We rush in?' he said.

'Yes, we're all real heroes here, aren't we?' said Evil Harry. 'No. That wasn't *exactly* what I had in mind. Lads, it's lucky for you that you've got me . . . '

It was the Chair of Indefinite Studies who saw the light on the moon. He was leaning on the ship's rail at the time, having a quiet afternoon smoke.

He was not an ambitious wizard, and generally just concentrated on keeping out of trouble and not doing anything very much. The nice thing about Indefinite Studies was that no one could describe exactly what they were. This gave him quite a lot of free time.

He watched the moon's pale ghost for a while, and then went and found the Archchancellor, who was fishing.

'Mustrum, should the moon be doing that?' he said.

Ridcully looked up. 'Good grief! *Stibbons!* Where's the man got to?'

Ponder was located in the bunk where he had flopped asleep fully dressed. He was hustled up the ladder half-asleep, but he awoke quickly when he saw the sky.

'Should it be doing that?' Ridcully demanded, pointing at the moon.

'No, sir! It certainly shouldn't!'

'It's a *definite* problem, is it?' said the Chair, hopefully.

'It certainly is! Where's the omniscope? Has anyone tried to talk to them?'

'Ah, well, not my field then,' said the Chair of Indefinite Studies, backing away. 'Sorry. Would help if I could. Can see you're busy. Sorry.'

All the dragons must have fired by now. Rincewind felt his eyeballs being pressed into the back of his head.

Leonard was unconscious in the next seat. Carrot was presumably lying in the debris that had been rammed to the other end of the cabin.

By the ominous creaking, and the smell, an orangutan was hanging on to the back of Rincewind's seat.

Oh, and when he managed to turn his head to see out of the window, one of the dragon pods was on fire. It was no wonder – the flame coming from the dragons was almost pure white.

Leonard had mentioned one of these levers . . . Rincewind stared at them through a red mist. 'If we have to drop all the dragons,' Leonard had said, 'we—' What? Which lever?

Actually, at a time like this the choice was plain.

Rincewind, his vision blurred, his ears insulted by the sound of a ship in pain, pulled the only one he could reach.

I can't put this in a saga, the minstrel thought. No one will ever believe it. I mean, they just won't ever *believe it* . . .

'Trust me, right?' said Evil Harry, inspecting the Horde. 'I mean, *yes*, obviously I am untrustworthy, point taken, but it's a matter of *pride* here, you understand? *Trust* me. This will *work*. I bet even the gods don't know *all* the gods, right?'

'I feel a right twerp with these wings,' Caleb complained.

'Mrs McGarry did a very good job on 'em, so don't complain,' snapped Evil Harry. 'You make a very good God of Love. What *kind* of love, I wouldn't like to say. And you are . . . ?'

'God of Fish, Harry,' said Cohen, who had stuck scales on his skin and made himself a sort of fish-head helmet from one of their late adversaries.

Evil Harry tried to breathe. 'Good, good, a very *old* fish god, yes. And you, Truckle, are . . . ?'

'The God of bloody Swearing,' said Truckle the Uncivil firmly.

'Er, that could actually work,' said the minstrel, as Evil Harry frowned. 'After all, there are Muses of dance and song, and there's even a Muse of erotic poetry—'

'Oh, I can do *that*,' said Truckle dismissively. '"There was a young lady from Quirm, Whose grip was—"'

'All right, all right. And you, Hamish?'

'God o' Stuff,' said Hamish.

'What stuff?'

Hamish shrugged. He hadn't survived all this time by being unnecessarily imaginative. 'Just . . . things, y'ken,' he said. 'Lost things, mebbe. Things lyin' aroound?'

The Silver Horde turned to the minstrel, who nodded after some thought.

'Could work,' he said, at last.

Evil Harry moved on to Boy Willie.

'Willie, why have you got a tomato on your head and a carrot in your ear?'

Boy Willie grinned proudly. 'You'll love this one,' he said. 'God of Bein' Sick.'

'It's been done,' said the minstrel, before Evil Harry could reply. 'Vometia. Goddess in Ankh-Morpork, thousands of years ago. "To give an offering to Vometia" meant to—'

'So you'd better think of something *else*,' growled Cohen.

'Oh? And what are *you* going to be, Harry?' said Willie.

'Me? Er . . . I'm going to be a Dark God,' said Evil Harry. 'There's a lot of them around—'

'Here, you never said we could be *demonic*,' said Caleb. 'If we can be *demonic*, I'm blowed if I'm gonna be a stupid cupid.'

'But if I'd said we could be demons you'd all have wanted to be demons,' Harry pointed out. 'An' we'd have been arguing for *hours*. Besides, the other gods're goin' to smell a rat if a whole *bunch* of dark gods turn up all at once.'

'Mrs McGarry hasn't done a *thing*,' said Truckle.

'Well, I thought if I could borrow Evil Harry's helmet I could slip in as a Valkyrie maiden,' said Vena.

'Good sensible thinkin',' said Evil Harry. 'There's bound to be a few of them around.'

'And Harry won't need it because in a minute he's going to make an excuse about his leg or his back or something and how he can't come in with us,' said Cohen, in a conversational voice. 'On account of him havin' betrayed us. Right, Harry?'

he game was getting more exciting. Most of the gods were watching now. Gods enjoy a good laugh, although it has to be said that their sense of humour is not subtle.

Blind Io, the elderly chief of the gods, said, 'I suppose there is no harm they can do us?'

'No,' said Fate, passing the dice box. 'If they were very intelligent, they would not be heroes.'

There was the rattle of a die, and one flew across the board and then began to spin in the air, tumbling faster and faster. Finally it vanished in a puff of ivory.

'Someone has thrown *uncertainty*,' said Fate. He looked along the table. 'Ah . . . my Lady . . .'

'My lord,' said the Lady. Her name was never spoken, although everyone knew what it was; speaking her name aloud would mean that she would instantly depart. Despite the fact that she had very few actual worshippers, she was nevertheless one of the most powerful of the deities on the Disc, since in their hearts nearly everyone hoped and believed that she existed.

'And what is your move, my dear?' said Io.

'I have already made it,' said the Lady. 'But I've thrown the dice where you can't see them.'

'Good, I like a challenge,' said Io. 'In that case—'

'If I may suggest a diversion, sir?' said Fate smoothly.

'And that is?'

'Well, they *do* want to be treated like gods,' said Fate. 'So I suggest we do so . . .'

'Are you thaying we thould take them *theriouthly*?' said Offler.

'Up to a point. Up to a point.'

'Up to which point?' said the Lady.

'Up the the point, madam, where it ceases to amuse.'

On the veldt of Howondaland live the N'tuitif people, the only tribe in the world to have *no imagination whatsoever*.

For example, their story about the thunder runs something like this: 'Thunder is a loud noise in the sky, resulting from the disturbance of the air masses by the passage of lightning.' And their legend 'How the Giraffe Got His Long Neck' runs: 'In the old days the ancestors of Old Man Giraffe had slightly longer necks than other grassland creatures, and the access to the high leaves was so advantageous that it was mostly long-necked giraffes that survived, passing on the long neck in their blood just as a man might inherit his grandfather's spear. Some say, however, that it is all a lot more complicated and this explanation only applies to the shorter neck of the okapi. And so it is.'

The N'tuitif are a peaceful people, and have been hunted almost to extinction by neighbouring tribes, who have lots of imagination, and therefore plenty of gods, superstitions and ideas about how much better life would be if they had a bigger hunting ground.

Of the events on the moon that day, the N'tuitif said: 'The moon was brightly lit and from

it rose another light which then split into three lights and faded. We do not know why this happened. It was just a thing.'

They were then wiped out by a nearby tribe who *knew* that the lights had been a signal from the god Ukli to expand the hunting ground a bit more. However, *they* were soon defeated entirely by a tribe who *knew* that the lights were their ancestors, who lived in the moon, and who were urging them to kill all non-believers in the goddess Glipzo. Three years later they in turn were killed by a rock falling from the sky, as a result of a star exploding a billion years ago.

What goes around, comes around. If not examined too closely, it passes for justice.

 n the shaking, rattling *Kite*, Rincewind watched the last two dragon pods drop from the wings. They tumbled alongside for a moment, broke up, and fell away.

He stared at the levers again. Someone, he thought muzzily, really should be doing *something* with them, shouldn't they?

 ragons contrailed across the sky. Now they were free of the pods, they were in a hurry to get home.

The wizards had created Thurlow's Interesting Lens just above the deck. The display was quite impressive.

'Better than fireworks,' observed the Dean.

Ponder banged on the omniscope. 'Ah, it's working now,' he said, 'but all I can see is this huge—'

More of Rincewind's face than a giant nose became visible as he drew back.

'What levers do I pull? What *levers* do I pull?' he screamed.

'What's happened?'

'Leonard's still out cold and the Librarian is pulling Carrot out of all the junk and this is definitely a bumpy ride! We've got no dragons left! What are all these dials for? I think we're falling! *What shall I do?*'

'Didn't you watch how Leonard did it?'

'He had his feet on two pedals and was pulling all the levers all the time!'

'All right, all right, I'll see if I can work out what to do from his plans and we can talk you down!'

'Don't! Talk me *Up*! *Up* is where we want to stay! Not down!'

'Are any of the levers marked?' said Ponder, scrabbling through Leonard's sketches.

'Yes, but I don't understand them! Here's one marked "Troba"!'

Ponder scanned the pages, covered in Leonard's backwards writing. 'Er . . . er . . . ' he muttered.

'Do *not* pull the lever marked "Troba"!' snapped Lord Vetinari, leaning forward.

'My lord!' said Ponder, and went red as Lord Vetinari's gaze fell upon him. 'I'm sorry, my lord, but this *is* rather technical, it is about *machinery*, and it would perhaps be better if those whose education had been more in the field of the arts did not . . . '

His voice faded under the Patrician's stare.

'This one's got a normal label! It's called "Prince Haran's Tiller"!' said a desperate voice from the omniscope.

Lord Vetinari patted Ponder Stibbons on the shoulder.

'I quite understand,' he said. 'The last thing a trained machinery person wants at a time like this is well-meant advice from ignorant people. I do apologise. And what is it that you intend to do?'

'Well, I, er, I . . .'

'As the *Kite* and all our hopes plunge towards the ground, I mean,' Lord Vetinari went on.

'I, er, I, let's see, we've tried . . .'

Ponder stared at the omniscope, and at his notes. His mind had become a huge, white, sticky field of hot fluff.

'I imagine we have at least a minute left,' said Lord Vetinari. 'No rush.'

'I, er, perhaps we, er . . .'

The Patrician leaned down towards the omniscope. 'Rincewind, pull Prince Haran's Tiller,' he said.

'We don't know what it does—' Ponder began.

'Do tell me if you have a better idea,' said Lord Vetinari. 'In the meantime, I suggest that the lever is pulled.'

On the *Kite*, Rincewind decided to respond to the voice of authority.

'Er . . . there's a lot of clicking and whirring . . .' he reported. 'And . . . some of the levers are moving by *themselves* . . . now the wings are unfolding . . . we're sort of flying in a straight line, at least . . . quite gently, really . . .'

'Good. I suggest you apply yourself to waking up Leonard,' said the Patrician. He turned and nodded at Ponder. 'You yourself have not studied the classics, young man? I know Leonard has.'

'Well . . . no, sir.'

'Prince Haran was a legendary Klatchian hero who sailed around the world on a ship with a magical tiller,' said Lord Vetinari. 'It steered the ship while he slept. If I can be of any further help, don't hesitate to ask.'

vil Harry stood frozen with terror as Cohen advanced across the snow, hand raised.

'You tipped off the gods, Harry,' said Cohen.

'We all *heard* yez,' said Mad Hamish.

'But it's *okay*,' Cohen added. 'Makes it more interestin'.' His hand came down and slapped the small man on the back.

'We thought: That Evil Harry, he may be dumber'n a thick brick, but betrayin' *us* at a time like this . . . well, that's what we call *nerve*,' said Cohen. 'I've known a few Evil Dark Lords in my time, Harry, but I'd def'nit'ly give you three great big goblins' heads for style. You might have never made it into the, you know, *big* Dark Lord league, but you've got . . . well, Harry, you've definitely got the Wrong Stuff.'

'We likes a man who sticks to his siege catapults,' said Boy Willie.

Evil Harry looked down and shuffled his feet, his face a battle between pride and relief.

'Good of you to say that, lads,' he mumbled. 'I mean, you know, if it was up to me I wouldn't do this to yer, but I got a reputation to—'

'I said we *understand*,' said Cohen. 'It's just like with us. You see a big hairy thing galloping towards you, you don't stop to think: Is this a rare species on the point of extinction? No, you hack its head off. 'Cos that's heroing, am I right? An' *you* see someone, you betray 'em, quick as wink, 'cos that's villaining.'

There was a murmur of approval from the rest of the Horde. In a strange way, this too was part of the Code.

'You're letting him *go*?' said the minstrel.

'Of course. You haven't been paying attention, lad. The Dark Lord *always* gets away. But you'd better put in the song that he betrayed us. That'll look good.'

'And . . . er . . . you wouldn't mind saying I fiendishly tried to cut your throats?' said Harry.

'All right,' said Cohen loftily. 'Put in that he fought like a black-hearted tiger.'

Harry wiped a tear from his eye. 'Thanks, lads,' he said. 'I don't know what to say. I won't forget this. This could turn things right round for me.'

'But do us a favour and see the bard gets back all right, though, will you?' said Cohen.

'Sure,' said Evil Harry.

'Um . . . I'm not going back,' said the minstrel.

This surprised everyone. It certain surprised him. But life had suddenly opened two roads in front of him. One of them led back to a life singing songs about love and flowers. The other could lead *anywhere*. There was something about these old men that made the first choice completely impossible. He couldn't explain it. That was just how it was.

'You've *got* to go back—' said Cohen.

'No, I've got to see how it ends,' said the minstrel. 'I must be mad, but that's what I want to do.'

'You can make that bit up,' said Vena.

'No, ma'am,' said the minstrel. 'I don't think I can. I don't think this is going to end in any way that I could make up. Not when I look at Mr Cohen there in his fish hat and Mr Willie as the God of Being Sick Again. No, I want to come along. Mr Dread can wait for me here. And I'll be perfectly safe, sir. No matter what. Because I'm absolutely *certain* that when the gods find they're under attack by a man with a tomato on his head and another one disguised as the Muse of Swearing they're really, *really* going to want the whole world to know what happened next.'

eonard was still out cold. Rincewind tried mopping his brow with a wet sponge.

'Of course I *watched* him,' said Carrot, glancing back at the gently moving levers. 'But he *built* it, so it was easy for him. Um . . . I shouldn't touch that, sir . . .'

The Librarian had swung himself into the driver's seat and was sniffing the levers. Somewhere underneath them, the automatic tiller clicked and purred.

'We're going to have to come up with some ideas soon,' Rincewind said. 'It won't fly itself for ever.'

'Perhaps if we gently . . . I shouldn't do that, sir—'

The Librarian gave the pedals a cursory glance. Then he pushed Carrot away with one hand while the other unhooked Leonard's flying goggles from their hook. His feet curled around the pedals. He pushed the handle that operated Prince Haran's Tiller and, far under his feet, something went *thud*.

Then, as the ship shook, he cracked his knuckles, reached out, waggled his fingers for a moment, and grabbed the steering column.

Carrot and Rincewind dived for their seats.

he gates of Dunmanifestin swung open, apparently by themselves. The Silver Horde walked inside, keeping together, peering around suspiciously.

'You better mark our cards for us, lad,' whispered Cohen, looking around the busy streets. 'I wasn't expecting *this*.'

'Sir?' said the minstrel.

'We expected a lot of carousing in a big 'all,' said Boy Willie. 'Not . . . *shops*. And everyone's different sizes!'

'Gods can be any size, I reckon,' said Cohen, as gods hurried towards them.

'Maybe we could . . . come back another time?' said Caleb.

The doors slammed behind them.

'No,' said Cohen.

And suddenly there was a crowd around them.

'You must be the *new* gods,' said a voice from the sky. 'Welcome to Dunmanifestin! You'd better come along with us!'

'Ah, the God of Fish,' said a god to Cohen, falling in beside him. 'And how *are* the fish, your mightiness?'

'Er . . . what?' said Cohen. 'Oh . . . er . . . wet. Still very wet. Very wet things.'

'And things?' a goddess asked Hamish. 'How *are* things?'

'Still lyin' aroond!'

'And are you omnipotent?'

'Aye, lass, but there's pills I'm takin' f'r it!'

'And you're the Muse of Swearing?' said a god to Truckle.

'Bloody right!' said Truckle desperately.

Cohen looked up and saw Offler the Crocodile God. He wasn't a god who was hard to recognise, but in any case Cohen had seen him many times before. His statue in temples throughout the world was a pretty good likeness, and now was the time for a man to reflect on the fact that so many of those temples had been left a good deal poorer as a result of Cohen's activities. He didn't, however, because it was not the kind of thing he ever did. But it did seem to him that the Horde was being hustled along.

'Where're we off to, friend?' he said.

'To watch the Gameth, your fithneth,' said Offler.

'Oh, yeah. That's where yo— *we* play around with u— mortals, right?' said Cohen.

'Yes, indeed,' said a god on the other side of Cohen. 'And currently we've found some mortals actually attempting to enter Dunmanifestin.'

'The devils, eh?' said Cohen pleasantly. 'Give 'em a taste of hot thunderbolt, that's my advice. It's the only language they understand.'

'Mostly because it's the only language you use,' mumbled the minstrel, eyeing the surrounded gods.

'Yes, we thought something like that would be a good idea,' said the god. 'I'm Fate, by the way.'

'Oh, *you're* Fate?' said Cohen, as they reached the gaming table. 'Always wanted to meet you. I thought you were supposed to be blind?'

'No.'

'How about if someone stuck two fingers in yer eyes?'

'I'm sorry?'

'Just my little joke.'

'Ha. Ha,' said Fate. 'I wonder, O God of Fish, how good a player *you* are?'

'Never been much of a gambler,' said Cohen, as a solitary die appeared between Fate's fingers. 'A mug's game.'

'Perhaps you would care for a little . . . venture?'

The crowd went silent. The minstrel looked into Fate's bottomless eyes, and knew that if you played dice with Fate the roll was always fixed.

You could have heard a sparrow fall.

'Yeah,' said Cohen, at last. 'Why not?'

Fate tossed the die on to the board. 'Six,' he said, without breaking eye contact.

'Right,' said Cohen. 'So I've got to a get a six too, yeah?'

Fate smiled. 'Oh, no. You are, after all, a god. And gods play to win. You, O mighty one, must throw a seven.'

'*Seven?*' said the minstrel.

'I fail to see why this should present a difficulty,' said Fate, 'to one entitled to be here.'

Cohen turned the die over and over. It had the regulation six sides.

'I could see that could present a difficulty,' he said, 'but only for mortals, o' course.' He

tossed the die up in the air once or twice. 'Seven?' he said.

'Seven,' said Fate.

'Could be a *knotty* one,' said Cohen.

The minstrel stared at him, and felt a shiver run down his spine.

'You'll remember I said that, lad?' Cohen added.

he *Kite* banked through high cloud.

'Ook!' said the Librarian happily.

'He flies it better than Leonard did!' said Rincewind.

'It must come more . . . easily,' whispered Carrot. 'You know . . . what with him being naturally atavistic.'

'Really? I've always thought of him as quite good-natured. Except when he's called a monkey, of course.'

The *Kite* turned again, curving through the sky like a pendulum.

'Ook!'

'"If you look out of the left window you can see practically everywhere",' Rincewind translated.

'Ook!'

'"And if you look out of the right window, you can see—" Good grief!'

There was the mountain. And there, glittering in the sunlight, was the home of the gods. Above it, just visible even in the brilliant air, was the shimmering misty funnel of the world's magical field earthing itself at the centre of the world.

'Are you, er, are you much of a religious man yourself?' said Rincewind as clouds whipped by the window.

'I believe all religions do reflect some aspect of an eternal truth, yes,' said Carrot.

'Good wheeze,' said Rincewind. 'You might just get away with it.'

'And you?' said Carrot.

'We-ll . . . you know that religion that thinks that whirling round in circles is a form of prayer?'

'Oh, yes. The Hurtling Whirlers of Klatch.'

'Mine is like that, only we go more in . . . straight lines. Yes. That's it. Speed is a sacrament.'

'You believe it gives you some sort of eternal life?'

'Not *eternal*, as such. More . . . well, just more, really. *More* life. That is,' Rincewind added, 'more life than you would have if you did *not* go very fast in a straight line. Although curving lines are acceptable in broken country.'

Carrot sighed. 'You're just a coward really, aren't you?'

'Yes, but I've never understood what's wrong with the idea. It takes guts to run away, you know. Lots of people would be as cowardly as me if they were brave enough.'

They looked out of the window again. The mountain was nearer.

'According to the mission notes,' said Carrot, thumbing through the sheaf of hastily written research notes that Ponder had thrust into his hand just before departure, 'a number of humans have entered Dunmanifestin in the past and returned alive.'

'Returned alive *per se* is not hugely comforting,' said Rincewind. 'With their arms and legs? Sanity? All minor extremities?'

'Mostly they were mythical characters,' said Carrot, uncertainly.

'Before or after?'

'The gods traditionally look favourably on boldness, daring and audacity,' Carrot went on.

'Good. You can go in first.'

'Ook,' said the Librarian.

'He says we'll have to land soon,' said Carrot. 'Was there some position we're supposed to get into?'

'Ook!' said the Librarian. He seemed to be fighting the levers.

'What do you mean, "lie on your back with your arms folded across your chest"?'

'Eek!'

'Didn't you watch what Leonard did when he landed us on the moon?'

'Ook!'

'And that was a *good* landing,' said Rincewind. 'Oh well, shame about the end of the world, but these things happen, eh?'

WOULD YOU LIKE A PEANUT? I AM AFRAID IT IS A LITTLE HARD TO GET THE PACKET OPEN.

A ghostly chair hung in the air next to Rincewind. A violet flaring round the edge of his vision told him that he was suddenly in a little private time and space of his own.

'So we *are* going to crash?' he said.

POSSIBLY. I'M AFRAID THE UNCERTAINTY PRINCIPLE IS MAKING MY JOB VERY DIFFICULT. HOW ABOUT A MAGAZINE?

The *Kite* curved around and began to glide gently towards the clouds aroud Cori Celesti. The Librarian glared at the levers, bit one or two of them, tugged the handle of Prince Haran's Tiller and then swung himself back along the cabin and hid under a blanket.

'We're going to land in that snowfield,' said Carrot, slipping into the pilot's seat. 'Leonard *designed* the ship to land in snow, didn't he? After all—'

The *Kite* did not so much land as kiss the snow. It bounced up into the air, glided a little further, and touched down again. There were a few more skips, and then the keel was running crisply and smoothly over the snowfield.

'Outstanding!' said Carrot. 'It's just a walk in the park!'

'You mean people are going to mug us and steal all our money and kick us viciously in the ribs?' said Rincewind. 'Could be. We're heading directly towards the city. Have you noticed?'

They stared ahead. The gates of Dunmanifestin were getting closer very quickly. The *Kite* breasted a snowdrift and sailed on.

'This is not the time to panic,' said Rincewind.

The *Kite* hit the snow, rebounded into the air and flew through the gateway of the gods.

Halfway through the gateway of the gods.

'So . . . seven and I win,' said Cohen. 'It comes down showin' seven and I win, right?'

'Yes. Of course,' said Fate.

'Sounds like a million-to-one chance to me,' said Cohen.

He tossed the die high in the air, and it slowed as it rose, tumbling glacially with a noise like the *swish* of windmill blades.

It reached the top of its arc and began to fall.

Cohen was staring fixedly at it, absolutely still. Then his sword was out of its scabbard and it whirled around in a complex curve. There was a *snick* and a green flash in the middle of the air and . . .

. . . two halves of an ivory cube bounced across the table.

One landed showing the six. The other landed showing the one.

One or two of the gods, to the minstrel's amazement, began to applaud.

'I think we had a deal?' said Cohen, still holding his sword.

'Really? And have you heard the saying "You cannot cheat Fate"?' said Fate.

Mad Hamish rose in his wheelchair. 'Ha' ye heard the sayin' "Can yer mither stitch, pal"?' he yelled.

As one man, or god, the Silver Horde closed up and drew its weaponry.

'No fighting!' shouted Blind Io. 'That is the rule here! We've got the *world* to fight in!'

'That wasn't cheating!' Cohen growled. 'Leavin' scrolls around to lure heroes to their death, *that's* cheatin'!'

'But where would heroes be without magic maps?' said Blind Io.

'Many of 'em 'd still be alive!' snapped Cohen. 'Not pieces in some damn game!'

'You *cut* the thing in *half*,' said Fate.

'Show me where it says that in the rules! Yeah, why not show me the *rules*, eh?' said Cohen, dancing with rage. 'Show me *all* the rules! What's up, Mr Fate? You want another go, is it? Double or quits? Double stakes?'

'You mutht admit it wath a good thtroke,' said Offler. Several of the lesser gods nodded.

'What? Are you prepared to let them stand here and *defy* us?' said Fate.

'Defy *you*, my lord,' said a new voice. 'I suggest they have won. He *did* cheat Fate. If you *do* cheat Fate, I do not believe it says anywhere that Fate's subsequent opinion matters.'

The Lady stepped daintily through the crowd. The gods parted to let her pass. They recognised a legend in the making when they saw it.

'And who are *you*?' snapped Cohen, still red with rage.

'I?' The Lady unfolded her hands. A die lay on each palm, the solitary single dot facing up. But at a flick of her wrist the two flew together, lengthened, entwined, became a hissing snake writhing in the air – and vanished.

'I . . . am the million-to-one-chance,' she said.

'Yeah?' said Cohen, less impressed than the minstrel thought he ought to be. 'And who are all the other chances?'

'I am those, also.'

Cohen sniffed. 'Then you ain't no lady.'

153

'Er, that's not really—' the minstrel began.

'Oh, that wasn't what I was supposed to say, was it?' said Cohen. 'I was supposed to say, "Ooh, ta, missus, much obliged"? Well, I ain't. They say fortune favours the brave, but *I* say I've seen too many brave men walkin' into battles they never walked out of. The hell with all of it— What's up with you?'

The minstrel was staring at a god on the edge of the crowd.

'It's *you*, isn't it?' he growled. 'You're Nuggan, aren't you?'

The little god took a step backward, but made the mistake of trying dignity. 'Be silent, mortal!'

'You utter, utter . . . fifteen years! Fifteen damn years before I ever tasted garlic! And the priests used to get up early in the countryside round us to jump on all the mushrooms! And do you know how *much* a small slab of chocolate cost in our town, and what they did to people who were caught with one?' The minstrel shouldered the Horde aside and advanced on the retreating god, his lyre raised like a club.

'I shall smite you with lightning!' squeaked Nuggan, raising his hands to protect himself.

'You can't! Not here! You can only do that stuff back in the world! All you can do here is bluff and illusion! And *bullying*! That's what prayers are . . . it's frightened people trying to make friends with the bully! All those temples were built and . . . and you're nothing but a little—'

Cohen laid a gentle hand on his shoulder. 'Well said, lad. Well said. But it's time you were goin'.'

'*Broccoli*,' murmured Offler to Sweevo, God of Cut Timber. '*You can't go wrong with broccoli.*'

'*I prohibit the practice of panupunitoplasty,*' said Sweevo.

'*What'th that?*'

'*Search me, but it's got them worried.*'

'Just let me give him one wallop—' shouted the minstrel.

'Listen, son, listen,' said Cohen, struggling to hold him. 'You got better things to do with that lyre than smash it over someone's head, right? A few little verses – it's 'mazin' how *they* stick in the mind. *Listen* to me, *listen*, do you hear what I'm tellin' you? . . . I've got a sword and it's a good one, but all the bleedin' thing can do is keep someone alive, *listen*. A song can keep someone *immortal*. Good or bad!'

The minstrel relaxed a little, but only a little. Nuggan had taken refuge behind a group of other gods.

'He'll wait until I'm out of the gates—' groaned the minstrel.

'He'll be busy! Truckle, press that plunger!'

'Ah, your famous firework,' said Blind Io. 'But, my dear mortal, fire cannot harm the gods . . .'

'Well now,' said Cohen, 'that depends, right? 'Cos in a minute or so, the top of this mountain is gonna look like a volcano. Everyone in the world will see it. I wonder if they'll believe in the gods any more?'

'Hah!' sneered Fate, but a few of the brighter gods looked suddenly thoughtful.

'Anyway,' Cohen went on, 'it dunt matter if someone *kills* the gods. It does matter that someone tried. Next time, someone'll try *harder*.'

'All that will happen is that *you* will be killed,' said Fate, but the more thoughtful gods were edging away.

'What have we got to lose?' said Boy Willie. 'We're going to die anyway. We're *ready* to die.'

'We've *always* been ready to die,' said Caleb the Ripper.

'That's why we've lived such a long time,' said Boy Willie.

'But . . . *why* be so upset?' said Blind Io. 'You've had long eventful lives, and the great cycle of nature—'

'Ach, the great cycle o' nature can eat ma loincloth!' said Mad Hamish.

'And there's not many as would want to do that,' said Cohen. 'And I ain't much good with words, but . . . I reckon we're doing this 'cos we *are* goin' to die, d'yer see? And 'cos some bloke got to the edge of the world somewhere and saw all them other worlds out there and burst into tears 'cos there was only one lifetime. So much universe, and so little time. And that's not right . . . '

But the gods were looking around.

The wings had shattered and broken off. The fuselage smashed down on to the cobbles, and slid on.

'*Now* is the time to panic,' said Rincewind. The stricken *Kite* continued to scrape across the flagstones in a growing smell of scorched wood.

A pale hand reached past Rincewind.

'It would be advisable,' said Leonard, 'to hold on to something.'

He pulled a small handle labelled 'Sekarb'.

Now the *Kite* stopped. In a very *dynamic* sort of way.

The gods looked down.

A hatch opened in the strange wooden bird. It fell off and rolled a little way.

The gods saw a figure get out. He appeared, in many ways, to be a hero, except that he was far too clean.

He looked around, removed his helmet and saluted.

'Good afternoon, O mighty ones,' he said. 'I do apologise, but this should not take long. And may I take this opportunity to say on behalf of the people of the Disc that you are doing a wonderful job here.'

He marched towards the Horde, past the astonished gods, and stopped in front of Cohen.

'Cohen the Barbarian?'

'What's it to you?' said Cohen, mystifed.

'I am Captain Carrot of the Ankh-Morpork City Watch, and I hereby arrest you on a charge of conspiracy to end the world. You need not say anything—'

'I don't *intend* to say anything,' said Cohen, raising his sword. 'I'm just gonna cut your —ing head off.'

'Hold it, hold it,' said Boy Willie urgently. 'Do you know who we all are?'

'Yessir. I believe so. You are Boy Willie, aka Mad Bill, Wilhelm the Chopper, the Great—'

'And *you* are going to arrest *us*? You say you are some kind of a watchman?'

'That is correct, sir.'

'We must've killed hundreds of watchmen in our time, lad!'

'I'm sorry to hear that, sir.'

''Ow much do they pay you, boy?' said Caleb.

'Forty-three dollars a month, Mr Ripper. With allowances.'

The Horde burst out laughing. Then Carrot drew his sword.

'I must insist, sir. What you are planning to do will destroy the world.'

'Only this bit, lad,' said Cohen. 'Now you could go off home and—'

'I'm being patient, sir, out of respect for your grey hairs.'

There was a further burst of laughing and Mad Hamish had to be slapped on the back.

'Just a moment, boys,' said Mrs McGarry quietly. 'Are we thinking this one through? Look around you.'

They looked around.

'Well?' Cohen demanded.

'There's me, and you,' said Vena, 'and Truckle and Boy Willie and Hamish and Caleb and the minstrel.'

'So? So?'

'That's seven,' said Vena. 'Seven of us, against one of him. Seven against one. And he thinks he's going to save the world. And he knows who we are and he's still going to fight us . . .'

'You think *he's* a hero?' cackled Mad Hamish. 'Hah! Wha' kind o' hero works for forty-three dollars a month? Plus allowances!'

But the cackle was all alone in the sudden quietness. The Horde could calculate the peculiar mathematics of heroism quite quickly.

There was, there *always* was, at the start and finish . . . the Code. They lived by the Code. You followed the Code, and you became part of the Code for those who followed *you*. The Code was *it*. Without the Code, you weren't a hero. You were just a thug in a loincloth.

The Code was quite clear. One brave man against seven . . . won. They knew it was true. In the past, they'd all *relied* on it. The higher the odds, the greater the victory. That was the Code.

Forget the Code, dismiss the Code, deny the Code . . . and the Code would *take* you.

They looked down at Captain Carrot's sword. It was short, sharp and plain. It was a working sword. It had no runes on it. No mystic gleam twinkled on its edge.

If you believed in the Code, that was worrying. One simple sword in the hands of a truly brave man would cut through a magical sword like suet.

It wasn't a frightening thought, but it *was* a thought.

'Funny thing,' said Cohen, 'but I heard tell once that down in Ankh-Morpork there's some watchman who's really heir to the throne but keeps very quiet about it because he *likes* being a watchman . . .'

Oh dear, thought the Horde. Kings in disguise . . . that was Code material, right there.

Carrot met Cohen's gaze.

'Never heard of him,' he said.

'To die for forty-three dollars a month,' said Cohen, holding the gaze, 'a man's got to be very, very stupid or very, *very* brave . . .'

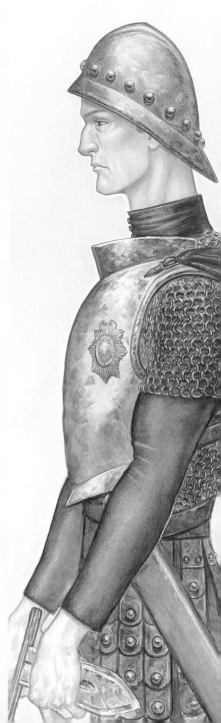

'What's the difference?' said Rincewind, stepping forward. 'Look, I don't want to break up a moment of drama or anything, but he's not joking. If that . . . keg explodes here, it *will* destroy the world. It'll . . . open a sort of hole and all the magic will drain away.'

'Rincewind?' said Cohen. 'What're *you* doing here, you old rat?'

'Trying to save the world,' said Rincewind. He rolled his eyes. '*Again*.'

Cohen looked uncertain, but heroes don't back down easily, even in the face of the Code. 'It'll *really* all blow up?'

'Yes!'

''S'not much of a world,' Cohen muttered. 'Not any more . . . '

'What about all the dear little kittens—' Rincewind began.

'Puppies,' hissed Carrot, not taking his eyes off Cohen.

'Puppies, I mean. Eh? Think of *them*.'

'Well. What about them?'

'Oh . . . nothing.'

'But everyone will die,' said Carrot.

Cohen shrugged his skinny shoulders. 'Everyone dies, sooner or later. So we're told.'

'There will be no one left to remember,' said the minstrel, as if he was talking to himself. 'If there's no one left alive, no one will remember.'

The Horde looked at him.

'No one will remember who you were or what you did,' he went on. 'There will be nothing. No more songs. *No one will remember*.'

Cohen sighed. 'All right, then let's say supposing I don't—'

'Cohen?' said Truckle, in an unusually worried voice. 'You know a few minutes ago, where you said "press the plunger"?'

'Yes?'

'You meant I shouldn't've?'

The keg was sizzling.

'You pressed it?' said Cohen.

'Well, *yes*! You *said*.'

'Can we stop it?'

'No,' said Rincewind.

'Can we outrun it?'

'Only if you can think of a way to run ten miles really, *really* fast,' said Rincewind.

'Gather round, lads! Not you, minstrel boy, this is *sword* stuff . . . ' Cohen beckoned the other heroes, and they went into a hurried huddle. It didn't seem to take long.

'Right,' said Cohen, as they straightened up. 'You got all our names down right, Mr Bard?'

'Of course—'

'Then let's go, lads!'

They heaved the keg back on to Hamish's wheelchair. Truckle half turned as they started to push it.

'Here, bard! You sure you made a note of that bit where I—?'

'We are *leaving!*' shouted Cohen, grabbing him. 'See you later, Mrs McGarry.'

She nodded, and stood back. 'You know how it is,' she said sadly. 'Great-grandchildren on the way and everything . . .'

The wheelchair was already moving fast. 'Get 'em to name one after me!' yelled Cohen as he leapt aboard.

'What're they doing?' said Rincewind as the chair rolled down the street towards the far gates.

'They'll never get it down from the mountain quickly enough!' said Carrot, starting to run.

The chair passed through the arch at the end of the street and rattled over the icy rocks.

As they hurried after it, Rincewind saw it bounce out and into ten miles of empty air. He thought he heard the last words, as the downward plunge began: 'Aren't we supposed to shout somethinggggg . . .'

Then chair and figures and barrel became smaller and smaller and merged into the hazy landscape of snow and sharp hungry rocks.

Carrot and Rincewind watched.

After a while the wizard noticed Leonard, out of the corner of his eye. The man had his fingers on his own pulse and was counting under his breath.

'Ten miles . . . hmm . . . allow for air resistance . . . call it three minutes plus . . . yes . . . yes, indeed . . . we should be averting our eyes around . . . yes . . . *now*. Yes, I think that would be a good i—'

Even through closed lids, the world went red.

When Rincewind crawled to the edge, he saw a small distant circle of evil black and crimson.

Several seconds later thunder boomed up the flanks of Cori Celesti, causing avalanches. And that, too, died away.

'Do you think they've survived?' said Carrot, peering down into the fog of dislodged snow.

'Huh?' said Rincewind.

'It wouldn't be the proper story if they didn't survive.'

'Captain, they fell about ten miles into an explosion which has just reduced a mountain to a valley,' said Rincewind.

'They could have landed in really deep snow on some ledge,' said Carrot.

'Or there may have been a passing flock of really large soft birds?' said Rincewind.

Carrot bit his lip. 'On the other hand . . . giving up their lives to save *everyone in the world* . . . that's a good ending, too.'

'But it was *them* who were going to blow it up!'

'Still very brave of them, though.'

'In a way, I suppose.'

Carrot shook his head sadly. 'Perhaps we could get down and check.'

'It's a great bubbling crater of boiling rock!' Rincewind burst out. 'It'd take a miracle!'

'There's always hope.'

'So? There's always taxes, too. It doesn't make any *difference*.'

Carrot sighed and straightened up. 'I wish you weren't right.'

'*You* wish I wasn't right? Come on, let's get back. We're not exactly out of trouble ourselves, are we?'

Behind them, Vena blew her nose and then tucked her handkerchief back into her armoured corset. It was time, she thought, to follow the smell of horses.

The remains of the *Kite* were the subject of keen but uncomprehending interest among the deitic classes. They weren't certain what it was, but they *definitely* disapproved of it.

'I feel,' said Blind Io, 'that if we had wanted people to fly, we would have given them wings.'

'We allow broomthtickth and magic carpeth,' said Offler.

'Ah, but they're magical. Magic . . . religion . . . there is a certain association. *This* is an attempt to subvert the natural order. Just *anyone* could float around the place in one of these things.' He shuddered. 'Men could look *down* upon their gods!'

He looked down upon Leonard of Quirm.

'Why did you do it?' he said.

'You gave me wings when you showed me birds,' said Leonard of Quirm. 'I just made what I saw.'

The rest of the gods said nothing. Like many professionally religious people – and they were pretty professional, being gods – they tended towards unease in the presence of the unashamedly spiritual.

'None of us recognise you as a worshipper,' said Io. 'Are you an *atheist?*'

'I think I can say that I definitely believe in the gods,' said Leonard, looking around. This seemed to satisfy everyone except Fate.

'And is that all?' he said. Leonard thought for a while.

'I think I believe in the secret geometries, and the colours on the edge of light, and the marvellous in everything,' he said.

'So you're not a religious man, then?' said Blind Io.

'I am a painter.'

'That's a "no", then, is it? I want to be clear on this.'

'Er . . . I don't understand the question,' said Leonard. 'As you ask it.'

'I don't think we understand the answers,' said Fate. 'As you give them.'

'But I suppose we owe you something,' said Blind Io. 'Never let it be said the gods are unjust.'

'We *don't* let it be said the gods are unjust,' said Fate. 'If I may suggest—'

'Will you be silent!' Blind Io thundered. 'We'll do it the the *old* way, thank you!'

He turned to the explorers and pointed a finger at Leonard.

'Your penalty,' said Blind Io, 'is this: you will paint the ceiling of the Temple of Small Gods in Ankh-Morpork. *All* of it. The decoration is in a terrible state.'

'But that's not *fair*,' said Carrot. 'He's not a young man, and it took the great Angelino Tweebsly twenty years to paint that ceiling!'

'Then it will keep his mind occupied,' said Fate. 'And prevent him thinking the wrong sort of thoughts. *That* is the correct punishment for those who usurp the powers of the gods! We will find work for idle hands to do.'

'Hmm,' said Leonard. 'A considerable amount of scaffolding . . . '

'*Vatht* amount,' said Offler, with satisfaction.

'And the nature of the painting?' said Leonard. 'I would like to paint . . . '

'The entire world,' said Fate. 'Nothing less.'

'Really? I was thinking of perhaps just a nice duck-egg blue with a few stars,' said Blind Io.

'The entire world,' said Leonard, staring off into some private vision. 'With elephants, and dragons, and the swirl of clouds, and mighty forests, and the currents of the sea, and birds, and the great yellow veldts, and the pattern of storms, and the crests of mountains?'

'Er, yes,' said Blind Io.

'Without assistance,' said Fate.

'Even with the thcaffolding,' said Offler.

'This is monstrous,' said Carrot.

Blind Io said: 'And if it is *not* completed in twenty years—'

'—ten years,' said Fate.

'—ten years, the city of Ankh-Morpork will be razed with heavenly fire!'

'Hmm, yes, good idea,' said Leonard, still staring at nothing. 'Some of the birds will have to be quite small . . . '

'He's in shock,' said Rincewind.

Captain Carrot had gone quiet with anger, as the sky does just before a thunderstorm.

'Tell me,' said Blind Io. 'Is there a god of policemen?'

'No, sir,' said Carrot. 'Coppers would be far too suspicious of anyone calling themselves a god of policemen to believe in one.'

'But you are a gods-fearing man?'

'What I've seen of them certainly frightens the life out of me, sir. And my commander always says, when we go about our business in the city, that when you look at the state of mankind you are forced to accept the reality of the gods.'

The gods smiled their approval of this, which was indeed an accurate quotation. Gods have little use for irony.

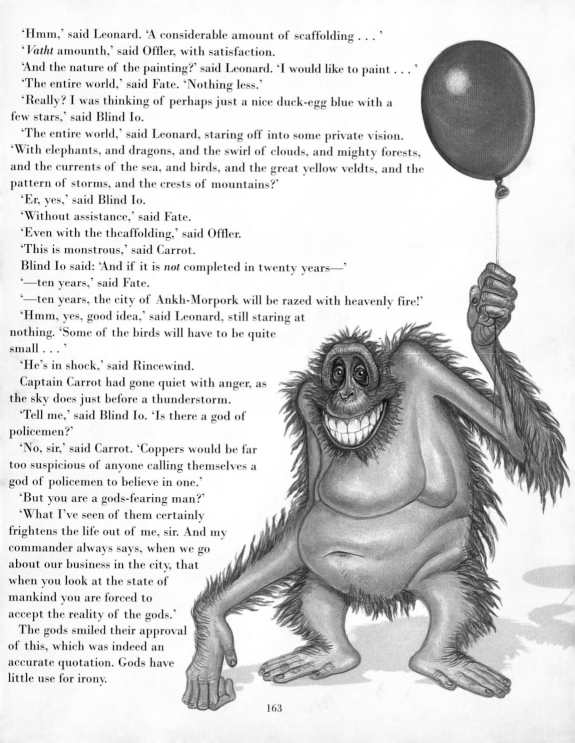

'Very good,' said Blind Io. 'And you have a request?'

'Sir?'

'Everyone wants something from the gods.'

'No, sir. I offer you an opportunity.'

'*You* will give something to *us*?'

'Yes, sir. A wonderful opportunity to show justice and mercy. I ask you, sir, to grant me a boon.'

There was silence. Then Blind Io said, 'Is that one of those . . . wooden objects, wasn't it? . . . with a handle, and . . . mmm . . . beads on one side, and a sort of . . . thing, with hooks on . . .' He paused. 'Did you mean one of those rubber things?'

'No, sir. That would be a balloon, sir. A boon is a request.'

'Is that all? Oh. Well?'

'Allow the *Kite* to be repaired so that we can go home—'

'Impossible!' said Fate.

'It sounds reasonable to me,' said Blind Io, glaring at Fate. 'It must be its last flight.'

'It *will* be the last flight of the *Kite*, won't it?' said Carrot to Leonard.

'Hmm? What? Oh, yes. Oh, certainly. I can see I designed a lot of it wrong. The *next* one – mmph . . .'

'What happened there?' said Fate suspiciously.

'Where?' said Rincewind.

'Where you clamped your hand over his mouth?'

'Did I?'

'You're still doing it!'

'Nerves,' said Rincewind, releasing his grip on Leonard. 'I've been a bit shaken up.'

'And do you want a boon too?' said Leonard.

'What? Oh. Er . . . I'd prefer a balloon, as a matter of fact. A blue balloon.' Rincewind gave Carrot a defiant look. 'It's all to do with when I was six, all right? There was this big unpleasant girl . . . and a pin. I don't want to talk about it.' He looked up at the watching gods. 'I don't know what everyone's staring at, I'm sure.'

'Ook,' said the Librarian.

'Does your pet want a balloon as well?' said Blind Io. 'We do *have* a monkey god if he wants some mangoes and so on . . .'

In the sudden chill, Rincewind said, 'In fact he said he wants three thousand file cards, a new stamp and five gallons of ink.'

'Eek!' said the Librarian, urgently.

'Oh, all right. And a red balloon too, please, if they're free.'

The repairing of the *Kite* was simple enough. Although gods, on the whole, do not feel at home around mechanical things, every pantheon everywhere in the universe finds it necessary to have some minor deity – Vulcan, Wayland, Dennis, Hephaistos – who knows how bits fit together and that sort of thing.

Most large organisations, to their regret and expense, have to have someone like that.

vil Harry surfaced from the snowdrift, and gasped for breath. Then he was plunged back down again by a firm hand.

'So it's a deal, then, is it?' said the minstrel, who was kneeling on his back and holding on to his hair.

Evil Harry rose again. 'Deal!' he roared, spitting snow.

'And if you tell me later that I shouldn't have listened to you because everyone knows Dark Lords can't be trusted, I'll garotte you with a lyre string!'

'You got no respect!'

'Well? You are an evil treacherous Dark Lord, right?' said the minstrel, pushing the spluttering head back into the snow.

'Well, yeah, of course . . . obviously. But respect costs nothi nnnn n n nn'.'

'You help me get down and I'll write you into the saga as the most wicked, iniquitous and depraved evil warlord there has even been, understand?'

The head came up again, wheezing.

'All right, all right. But you gotta promise . . . '

'And if you betray me, remember that I don't know the Code! I don't have to let Dark Lords get away!'

They descended in silence and, in Harry's case, mostly with his eyes shut.

Off to one side and a long way down, a foothill that was now a valley still fumed and bubbled.

'We'd never even find the bodies,' said the minstrel, as they sought for a path.

'Ah, and that'd be 'cos they didn't die, see?' said Harry. 'They'd have come up with some plan at the last minute, you can bet on it.'

'Harry—'

'You can call me Evil, lad.'

'Evil, they spent the last minute falling down a mountain!'

'Ah, but maybe they kind of *glided* through the air, see? And there's all those lakes down there. Or maybe they spotted where the snow was *really* deep.'

The minstrel stared. 'You really think they could have *survived?*' he said.

There was a slight touch of desperation in Harry's raddled face.

'Sure. O' course. All that talk from Cohen . . . that was just talk. He's not the sort to go around dyin' all the time. Not old Cohen! I mean . . . not *him*. 'E's one of a kind.'

The minstrel surveyed the Hublands ahead of him. There *were* lakes and there *was* deep snow. But the Horde was not in favour of cunning. If they needed cunning, they hired it. Otherwise, they simply attacked. And you couldn't attack the ground.

It's all mixed up, he thought. Just like that captain said. Gods and heroes and wild adventure . . . but when the last hero goes, it all goes.

He'd never been keen on heroes. But he realised that he needed them to be there, like forests and mountains . . . he might never see them, but they filled some sort of hole in his mind. Some sort of hole in everyone's mind.

'Bound to be fine,' said Evil Harry, behind him. 'They'll probably be waitin' for us when we get down there.'

'What's that, hanging on that rock?' said the minstrel.

It turned out, when they'd scrambled up to it over slippery rocks, to be part of a shattered wheel from Mad Hamish's wheelchair.

'Doesn't mean nothing,' said Evil Harry, tossing it aside. 'Come on, let's get a move on. This is not a mountain you want to be on at night.'

'No. You're right. It doesn't,' said the minstrel. He unslung his lyre and began to tune it. 'It doesn't mean *anything*.'

Before he turned to leave, he reached into a ragged pocket and pulled out a small leather bag. It was full of rubies.

He tipped them out on to the snow, where they glowed. And then he walked on.

There was a field of deep snow. Here and there a hollow suggested that the snow had been thrust aside with great force by a falling body, but the edges had been softened by the wind drift.

The seven horsewomen landed gently, and the thing about the snow was this: there were hoofprints in it, but they did not appear *exactly* where the horses trod or exactly *when* they did. They seemed superimposed on the world, as if they had been drawn first and the artist did not have much time to paint the reality behind them.

168

They waited for a while.

'Well, this is jolly unsatisfactory,' said Hilda (soprano). 'They ought to *be* here. They do know they're dead, don't they?'

'We haven't come to the wrong place, have we?' said Gertrude (mezzo-soprano).

'Ladies? If you would be so kind as to dismount?'

They turned. The seventh Valkyrie had drawn her sword and was smiling at them.

'What cheek. Here, you're not Grimhilda!'

'No, but I think I could probably beat all six of you,' said Vena, tossing aside the helmet. 'I shoved her in the privy with one hand. It would be . . . *better* if you simply dismounted.'

'Better? Better than what?' said Hilda.

Mrs McGarry sighed. 'This,' she said.

The snow erupted old men.

'Evening, miss!' said Cohen, grabbing Hilda's bridle. 'Now, are you goin' to do like she says, or shall I get my friend Truckle here to ask you? Only he's a bit . . . uncivil.'

'Hur, hur, hur!'

'How dare you—'

'I'll dare anything, miss. Now get off or I'll push yer off!'

'Well, really!'

'Excuse me? I say? Excuse me?' said Gertrude. 'Are you *dead*?'

'Are we dead, Willie?' said Cohen.

'We *ought* be be dead. But I don't *feel* dead.'

'I ain't dead!' roared Mad Hamish. 'I'll knock any man doon as tells me a'm dead!'

'There's an offer you can't refuse,' said Cohen, swinging himself on to Hilda's horse. 'Saddle up, boys.'

'But . . . excuse me?' said Gertrude, who was one of those people afflicted with terminal politeness. 'We were supposed to take you to the great Halls of the Slain. There's mead and roast pork and fighting in between courses! Just for you! That's what you *wanted*! They laid it on *just for you*!'

'Yeah? Thanks all the same, but we ain't goin',' said Cohen.

'But that's where dead heroes have got to go!'

'I don't remember signin' anythin',' said Cohen. He looked up at the sky. The sun had set, and the first stars were coming out. Every one was a world, eh? 'You still not joining us, Mrs McGarry?' he said.

'Not yet, boys.' Vena smiled. 'Not quite ready, I think. There'll come a time.'

'Fair enough. Fair enough. We'll be going, then. Got a lot to do . . . '

'But—' Mrs McGarry looked across the snowfield. The wind had blown the snow over . . . shapes. Here a sword hilt projected from a drift, there a sandal was just visible. 'Are you dead or not?' she said.

Cohen scanned the snow. 'Well, the way I see it, we don't *think* we are, so why should we care what anyone else thinks? We never have. Ready, Hamish? Then follow me, boys!'

Vena watched as the Valkyries, squabbling among themselves, made their way back to the mountain. Then she waited. She had a feeling that there would be something to wait for.

After a while, she heard another horse whinny.

'Are you collecting?' she said, and turned to look at the mounted figure.

THAT IS SOMETHING ABOUT WHICH I DO NOT PROPOSE TO ENLIGHTEN YOU, said Death.

'But you *are* here,' said Vena, although now she felt a lot more like Mrs McGarry again. Vena would probably have killed a few of the horsewomen just to make sure the others paid attention, but they'd all looked so *young*.

I AM, OF COURSE, EVERYWHERE.

Mrs McGarry looked up at the stars.

'In the olden days,' she said, 'when a hero had been really heroic, the gods would put them up in the stars.'

THE HEAVENS CHANGE, said Death. WHAT TODAY LOOKS LIKE A MIGHTY HUNTER MAY LOOK LIKE A TEACUP IN A HUNDRED YEARS' TIME.

'That doesn't seem fair.'

NO ONE EVER SAID IT HAD TO BE. BUT THERE ARE OTHER STARS.

t the base of the mountain, at Vena's camp, Harry got the fire going again while the minstrel sat and picked out notes.

'I want you listen to this,' he said, after a while, and played something.

It went on, it seemed to Evil Harry, for a lifetime.

He wiped away a tear as the last notes died away.

'I've got to do some more work on it,' said the minstrel, in a faraway voice. 'But will it do?'

'You asking me *will it do?*' said Evil Harry. 'You're telling me you think you could make it even *better?*'

'Yes.'

'Well, it's not like . . . a real saga,' said Evil Harry hoarsely. 'It's got a *tune*. You could whistle it, even. Well, hum it. I mean, it even *sounds* like them. Like they'd sound if they was music . . .'

'Good.'

'It's . . . wonderful . . .'

'Thank you. It will get better as more people hear it. It's music for people to listen to.'

'And . . . it's not like we found any bodies, is it?' said the very small Dark Lord. 'So they could be alive *somewhere*.'

The minstrel picked a few notes on the lyre. The strings shimmered. 'Somewhere,' he agreed.

'Y'know, kid,' said Harry, 'I don't even know your name.'

The minstrel's brow wrinkled. He wasn't certain himself, any more. And he didn't know where he was going to go, or what he was going to do, but he suspected that life might be a lot more interesting from now on.

'I'm just the singer,' he said.

'Play it again,' said Evil Harry.

incewind blinked, stared, and then looked away from the window.

'We've just been overtaken by some men on horseback,' he said.

'Ook,' said the Librarian, which probably meant, 'Some of us have got some flying to do.'

'I just thought I'd mention it.'

Spiralling through the air like a drunken clown, the *Kite* climbed the column of hot air from the distant crater. It was the only instruction Leonard had given before going and sitting so quietly at the back of the cabin that Carrot was getting seriously worried.

'He just sits there whispering things like "ten years!" and "the whole world!",' he reported. 'It's come as a terrible shock. What a penance!'

'But he looks *cheerful*,' said Rincewind. 'And he keeps drawing sketches. And he's leafing through all those pictures you took on the moon.'

'Poor chap. It's affecting his mind.' Carrot leaned forward. 'We ought to get him home as soon as possible. What's the usual direction? "Second star to the left and straight on 'til morning"?'

'I think that may very probably be the stupidest piece of astronavigation ever suggested,' said Rincewind. 'We're just going to head for the lights. Oh, and we'd better be careful not to look down on the gods.'

Carrot nodded. 'That's quite hard.'

'Practically impossible,' said Rincewind.

nd in a place on no map the immortal Mazda, bringer of fire, lay on his eternal rock.

Memory can play tricks after the first ten thousand years, and he wasn't quite sure what had happened. There had been some old men on horseback, who'd swooped out of the sky. They'd cut his chains, and given him a drink, and had taken it in turns to shake his withered hand.

Then they'd ridden away, into the stars, as quickly as they'd come.

Mazda lay back into the shape his body had worn into the stone over the centuries. He wasn't quite sure about the men, or why they'd come, or why they'd been so happy. He was only sure, in fact, about two things.

He was sure it was nearly dawn.

He was sure that he held, in his right hand, the very sharp sword the old men had given him.

And he could hear, coming closer with the dawn, the beat of an eagle's wings.

He was going to *enjoy* this.

It is in the nature of things that those who save the world from certain destruction often don't get hugely rewarded because, since the certain destruction does not take place, people are uncertain how certain it may have been and are, therefore, somewhat tight when it comes to handing out anything more substantial than praise.

The *Kite* was landed rather roughly on the corrugated surface of the river Ankh and, as happens to public things lying around which don't appear to belong to anyone, quickly became the private property of many, many people.

And Leonard began the penance for his hubris. This was much approved of by the Ankh-Morpork priesthood. It was definitely the sort of thing to encourage piety.

Lord Vetinari was therefore surprised when he received an urgent message three weeks after the events recounted, and forced his way through the mob to the Temple of Small Gods.

'What's going on?' he demanded of the priests peering around the door.

'This is . . . blasphemy!' said Hughnon Ridcully.

'Why? What has he painted?'

'It's not what he's painted, my lord. What he's painted is . . . is amazing. *And he's finished it!*'